IN ALL PROBABILITY

A Collection of Short Stories

Steve Morris

PNEUMA SPRINGS PUBLISHING UK

First Published in 2009 by:
Pneuma Springs Publishing

In all Probability
Copyright © 2009   Steve Morris
ISBN: 978-1-905809-43-1

This is a work of fiction. Names, characters, places and incidents are either products of the author's imagination or are used fictitiously. Any resemblance to actual events or locales or persons, living or dead, save those clearly in the public domain, is purely coincidental.

Pneuma Springs Publishing
A Subsidiary of Pneuma Springs Ltd.
7 Groveherst Road, Dartford Kent, DA1 5JD.
E: admin@pneumasprings.co.uk
W: www.pneumasprings.co.uk

A catalogue record for this book is available from the British Library.

Published in the United Kingdom. All rights reserved under International Copyright Law. Contents and/or cover may not be reproduced in whole or in part without the express written consent of the publisher.

IN ALL PROBABILITY

Introduction

This book deliberately contains no heroes. The world does not revolve around heroes. It revolves around real people who sometimes find themselves in seemingly unreal situations. When we sympathise with the characters within these stories and with the ways that fate deals with them, we sympathise with ourselves.

Some of the characters and events in these stories are based on real people and situations I have met along my way.

A few of these stories were first penned in my teenage years. Fate gave me an opportunity to type some of them up into this first book.

Allow me to present to you my first volume of short stories. Have a quick read while you can. Be quick, though. In all probability, Lady Luck will soon toss something life-changing out of the sky right into your lap just to see how you handle it. She usually does.

Steve Morris

2009

Contents

1. Dead-Eye 7
2. Lightning Strikes Twice 12
3. The Lay-Off 16
4. My Tune 21
5. Older Not Wiser 24
6. If I could Bottle It 28
7. All Around Us 33
8. Life's Too Short 38
9. Shared House 42
10. Three Strikes and you're out 46
11. The Best Days of our Lives 50
12. Revenge on a plate 54
13. Better Late than Never 57
14. The Brand New Colour 60
15. Dreamer 64
16. Enchantment 67
17. Quiet Life 72
18. Perfect 75
19. If Only 80
20. It's an ill wind 83
21. Let the good times roll 87
22. Memories are made of this 90
23. Potential Energy 93
24. The Remainder 97
25. Voices 100
26. Winston Churchill 103
27. Signal 107
28. Swan Song 109
29. Progress 114
30. Acquired Taste 117

Steve Morris

"Dead Eye"

We'd never seen anyone throw a ball like that. Blew the bails off the cricket stumps from a full hundred yards. Easy. No fluke. He did it again and again then walked away bored. He could do it for fun and could have done it all day long if he had wanted to. He was just a kid. If they could have got him to behave, the teachers would have had a national talent on their hands for sure. We were privileged, as he usually didn't join in games unless he felt like it. Teachers tried to get him involved in all sorts of sports. Sadly, as he was hardly ever there and not remotely bothered about his education, the system never really had much chance with him.

I remember him playing in the woods with us once one summer. He just appeared randomly one day and casually just joined in, as he did. Dark-haired, with darker eyelashes, freckled and always a little scruffy; he had a type of cult status even at his tender age. He was always just a little too arrogant to be likeable but we let him join in with our games if he ever felt like it. We knew little about his family. This boy didn't seem to have a permanent group of friends but, due to his skills, was never short of company when he wanted it.

In those woods, we were throwing all sorts of things at each other all that day and went home filthy, as kids did back then. I remember him picking some little fishing weights from his pocket. We all knew what he could do but he was getting better and better every time we saw him. Amazingly, while we were sat talking, he took a rook out of a tree quite easily. Fair enough, but shortly after that he cruelly hit one of them in mid-flight, and as hard as any catapult. Like I said, we had never seen anything like it. Another time, we saw him practicing his trade alone on the beach. It was, for him a typically solitary self-taught training session. Who could he practice with? He had carefully made a tall pile of smooth flat stones, and then went about demolishing it with projected pebbles from carefully paced positions farther and farther out, as if daring himself to test the limits of his own developing talent further with each subsequent throw. He took his time. The routine involved him standing casually, one leg a shoulder's width in front of the other in line with the target, then staring intently with one eye almost closed, before raising his right arm. Some of the shots from way off curved dramatically inwards before splattering the pile of rocks in all directions with a piercingly clean crack. Sometimes it took two throws to completely destroy all traces of the pile but they never seemed to miss. As if drawn in magnetically from their trajectory, the stones hit home like this boy could read the very wind itself. We rarely ever used his real name. Everyone called him "Dead-Eye" for obvious reasons.

When we were about 13 years old, and before we realised someone was missing, he must have left our school and moved elsewhere as we never really saw much of him again. We had other things to do at that age and forgot all about "Dead-Eye". All of us meet memorable kids at school but often soon forget about them after we leave those days behind to get on with our own emerging lives. Occasionally they come back into our mind when we least expect it. Rather than bump into him in some supermarket twenty years later, in the case of Dead Eye, he would bizarrely turn up again in just about as big a way as was possible.

All of a sudden, he was in a news story that was to receive massive round-the clock world media coverage. Although the story had been running for a day or so before I had picked up on it, I soon found myself engrossed in remembering those supposedly innocent childhood days sat killing summer holiday time with this small freckled kid. I recognised his face instantly in the newspapers and on TV. As always in these cases, they had got hold of our school class photo.

There had been an assassination. It was a big one this time. Al-Sadir, an influential Al-Q'aeda leader had been audaciously "taken out" on live television right in front of hundreds of his own supporters. In the war against terror, it was long overdue. The American President could hardly contain his jubilation and he visibly beamed at press conferences.

Al-Sadir had been the scourge of US anti-terror efforts for five years. Despite the very best efforts of the US and UK governments, Al-Sadir managed to arrogantly spin the media even here in the West with his smug weekly rogue Satellite TV broadcasts. Using the very latest technology the USA spent millions trying to trace, jam and destroy these propaganda signals to no avail. There was always at least one TV channel that managed to broadcast them. The leader bragged about his group's successful acts of terror carried out against the US "Leviathan", and taunted the West with talk of their intended future targets. Al-Sadir was a digital-age contemporary of Lord Haw Haw. Something just had to be done.

According to media sources, it seemed that a young man with a remarkable skill had drifted into the army some time in his twenties. A unique talent at baseball, juggling and darts throwing had resulted in him being quickly noticed. Special Forces training soon followed with both the UK and US military. Then came much work on his appearance so he could blend into undercover operations. Apparently he had been specially trained as an assassin for covert counter-terror situations where no one else could ever get. The press went on to speculate about his background. They knew very little. They tried to suggest a previous circus family background in knife throwing and tried to tie the story in with several high-profile rebel leaders who had been mysteriously "taken-out" in the last few years. This of course was quite plausible. Behind the headlines, I actually knew what this man could do.

Al-Sadir, given his growing influence in the world stage was always surrounded by a massive security operation and had several doubles. His exact locations and movements between the broadcasts were kept very secret. Every member of his frenzied adoring crowd of supporters was frisked thoroughly before their leader would appear in front of them.

"Dead-Eye" didn't need a knife. He didn't need a rifle, pistol or grenade. He didn't need to have explosives strapped around his body. "Dead-Eye" only needed a stone. They could have searched him all day long for all he cared. No metal detector would ever bleep. They wouldn't find anything of interest on him. His deadly weapon could be easily smuggled, if necessary, in something like a piece of bread. In this dry, dusty and stony environment, he could have held a murder weapon in his hand for everyone to see.

His coaching had been extensive. "Dead-Eye" knew exactly where to aim on the back of his target's head to get the correct brain injury. Casual as ever, he knew he wouldn't get the chance for a second throw, but was always confident he would not need one. He was sure about this one. If "Dead-Eye's" impact was two centimetres off his intended position, he would have been disappointed. He had been trained. Al-Sadir must not be allowed to recover from this injury. "Kill him or vegetate him, then get out quietly" was his brief. Special Forces had tried to get other assassins close to this guy before but had never got anyone near. It was a rare opportunity.

Arriving at the scene early, he blended in without a problem. Weapon selection had been some days before. Confidently and arrogantly, "Dead-Eye" fingered his stone in his pocket for some time. He spiralled it between his thumb and the first two fingers of his right hand to get the most comfortable grip. He felt the weight again and again. The stone was warm and a little moist. There was a lot of money in this one. He casually looked around to finalise his escape route. The assassin had positioned himself high on a wall at the back of the crowd. He then held his arms behind his head for about ten minutes so no one would notice an arm being raised immediately before the despatch. He would be all right. There would be no smoke, no recoil and no shot noise. There never was. His biggest danger was of him being seen acting suspiciously. The pace of the speech increased. Everyone's eyes were tunnelled on Al-Sadir, hanging on to his every word.

Al-Sadir turned momentarily away from the crowd. The time had come.

The stone splattered quietly into the rear of his head. The leader fell silently to his knees. From the moment that stone left Dead-Eye's fingers it was a winner. Weighted beautifully, there was just the right measured spin on that one. Dead-Eye instantly turned in the split second of the red liquid impact on Al-Sadir's skull. It was a good clean hit. The assassin slowly levered both his legs over the wall while stretching both arms out high as if continuing a yawn. Hardly anyone had realised that Al-Sadir was now about to die of brain injuries. Thinking that he had stumbled on the camera wire, people carried on watching oblivious. The leader did not get back to his feet. The leader was in big trouble.

Supporters ran to surround the jerking body of Al-Sadir. Soon, the crowd was panicking. Rifles were being fired. The TV cameras were hastily turned away from their leader. Screams began to ring out. Dead-Eye merged stealthily into the background and slowly, step-by-step, was moving away from his place of work. He had begun thoughts even of his next job.

A foot was across his shins. A stick was in his back. Hands were around his throat. He was being dragged toward the guards.

Someone had seen.

The broadcasts began again the next day. Al-Sadir was portrayed as a martyr. Successors were appointed. Much was made that the assassin had been captured alive. The trial was delayed to give the Western newspapers enough time for Dead-Eye's bruised prisoner photograph to reach the breakfast table of every household.

His brutal interrogation and subsequent trial was deliberately televised. The scenes were played out live on Satellite television into every UK and USA home over the following few days. People were transfixed. Dead-Eye was to be used in propaganda against the West and an example was to be made of him. This terror group were ironically now getting more airtime than ever. With the jerkily handheld cameras that often focused closely on his blackened face, came the moment I recognised his dark hair, eyes and freckles once again and thought back to the lonely boy on the beach. The footage was interspersed with "highlights" of Al-Sadir's best speeches. It was not a long trial.

Under their law, the punishment was deemed to fit the crime. The sentence was to be the death penalty. The execution itself was to be broadcast live in front of the cameras.

It was to be death by stoning.

"Lightning Strikes Twice"

People sometimes wondered what ever happened to Julian Villette the singer. Little enough was known of the star before his fame. Even less was known about his subsequent ordinary life under his even more ordinary name of Malcolm Davies. What we did all know about him, however, was that he was the man behind that massive memorable 70s disco hit "Lightning Strikes Twice". Everyone who had been on holiday anywhere that summer knew that one. The bars and nightclubs were full of it and even the kids loved it. There was no avoiding the risqué "Lightning" with its shallow chauvinistic lyric about one man's conquests. It became inseparably synonymous with that long hot August.

Julian Villette paraded his dance on Top of the Pops dressed in leather trousers, long brown leather trench coat and his almost-as-long hair. The song was huge for its short life span. It was his first and only hit record. Like so many other singers with massive hits that had become far too massive for their own good; soon after, he disappeared into thin air. For those disposable artists, their first song gets so very big that no matter how much better the follow-up song was, it would always be seen as an anti-climax. Such was the success of "Lightning Strikes Twice" that Julian Villette was advised to not even bother trying to record a follow-up single. According to the press articles of the time, he didn't need to. They said that he was already mega-rich and had wine, women, sports cars and a life of luxury ahead of him. Or at least so people were led to believe. For Malcolm Davies however, none of this was actually true. It was all hype released by the record company at the time. Someone had obviously made money out of "Lightning" but it wasn't him. He had a tiny royalty on a "one record" deal and very little else. Singles themselves never made a lot in those days. The real money was made with albums and tours. After his chart success, he was not a rich man; he owned neither mansion, nor sports cars, had no family and was not particularly happy. Relationships were difficult to form for Malcolm because women were reluctant to trust him; such was his reputation from the song. Oh yes, he had plenty of offers at that time. However, they always were from the wrong type of woman for church-going Malcolm. They were from those types of women that he always disliked. Judging by the lyric of "Lightning", those particular women would have been ideal for Julian Villette. He thought he had found some happiness briefly. He set his heart on only one girl called Mary who was working for the record company helping to promote the single during a Spanish tour that summer. All sunglasses, scarves, tied-back long hair and safari shorts; Mary was an outstanding example of the very best seventies jet-set glamour. She was the one for him and he fell in love all too quickly. Mary would not have been out of place alongside any stylist celebrity of the time. She was instantly attracted by Malcolm and spent time working closely with him but was soon put off by all his female attention and by the continually intrusive press stories surrounding the supposed antics of his alter ego. No matter how much he tried to persuade her of his previous church-going background, she was convinced that he actually was a Julian Villette character. He took Mary's rejection very seriously and it was to remain deeply within him. He became bitter about relationships and decided to give up on them.

Twenty-five years down the line and things were not much different. Malcolm's life was not particularly much of one. He had moved around the country, being unable to settle anywhere. Everything in life was always going to be an anti-climax after his short burst of fame all those years ago. He was an untidy man who lived in an even untidier flat. His neighbours neither knew him, nor knew of him nor cared to know of him.

Drink was Malcolm's recurrent problem in those years afterwards. He kept quiet about his past life and tried to forget it. He now lived and worked in his own quiet routine as a warehouseman in a large supermarket. This, together with the odd small royalty cheque helped to pay the bills. Apparently Malcolm had "signed away" the rights to the song so anyone could cover it if they should wish to. He never actually remembered doing that but it explained why he was unable to stop "Talent-less morons" regularly destroying the song on piped musak CDs. However, he would still receive a small royalty from each CD sold so it wasn't totally a bad thing.

Occasionally the song was used on a few of those retro compilation albums. Particularly annoying was when some exceptionally bland piped supermarket singer had completely murdered the song on a summer CD alongside other seventies' "novelty" songs. One of these was piped into the supermarket ad nauseum throughout all of last July and August so he had to repeatedly endure "the thing" during his work. Malcolm even tried to change to the night shift to avoid having to listen to it. He decided that he had always hated "Lightning Strikes Twice".

Then came a Saturday morning with a phone call from a representative from a record company. "I've been trying to track you down for ages Mr Davies...You still got that hair, by the way?..... Anyway, Listen...you don't keep up with the charts much these days do you?" the record company guy assumed rather than asked. ". Well then, you won't have heard the news. Did you know that girl-group Buzz-Whack have sampled your song on a track on their new album? The track itself was released as a single on Monday and I'll tell you- the kids just can't get enough... I'll be in touch"

The best part of the riff had been sped up, and played under a bombastic synth-loop that worked an absolute treat. Malcolm found it difficult to admit, but he actually really liked it. They had really improved the song. Also the royalties would come in very useful. He then started listening to the radio again! At work, he tapped his feet when he heard Buzz-Whack on a lorry's radio. He untied his ponytail and washed his hair.

A couple of weeks later the record company guy was on the phone again. "Listen...any chance of sorting yourself out Mr Davies? Got any of that old gear? Everyone's asking for you....'What happened to Villette?' is all we're getting. I'm telling you... if we re-release it as a single in the next month or so we're minted....It'll need a little re-mixing for the current market, mind"

Malcolm had a feeling that he had little choice in the matter. The money would come in useful. Record deals were different nowadays. The clothes were all rotted away or else previously thrown away. The long hair was fortunately all still there but needed dying. Re-learning the words wasn't difficult. He had been trying to forget them for twenty-five years. Cigarettes had taken their toll on his voice but apparently he would only have to mine the song live.

He was surprised how quickly the CD took to record, mix and produce. It soon began to get mainstream airplay and the press were gathering. This time he got a lawyer to check through the record contract.

Within a month he had gone from Saturday mornings watching TV lying in bed to Saturday mornings in a TV studio. He was in his element. As Malcolm became Julian Villette once more, his confidence returned. He looked everyone in the eye. He walked and talked differently. He began to notice women and they began to notice him. The rehearsal tension, the smells from the make-up and the heat from the studio lights all combined to a magic instant when it was summer 1978 all over again. Villette was the centre of the world.

A confectionary company simultaneously began using the song as a soundtrack to a ubiquitous TV campaign. He couldn't lose.

As "Lightning" began to rise in the charts Malcolm found that he was invited out most nights of the week. He met many new people. This time he was more generally more wary and avoided any women remotely connected to the music industry.

Malcolm, perhaps unusually for a pop star, began to re-attend Church events. This was something he had not done for a long time. People obviously knew who he was but he modestly avoided talking about lightning. This was to be a new beginning for him. He realised that he should have done this all before.

He soon became attracted to a travel agent called Sheila. She was a similar age to Malcolm. Apparently she had once been a fashion model. It was the overall way that she carried herself that caught Malcolm's attention quickly. He imagined that she must have really been something special in "her day". She admitted that she didn't actually remember the first time that the record was in the charts. That was good. The future was all that mattered. Malcolm considered his advancing years, his previously wasted opportunities and his second chance for happiness and resolved to make pro-active attempts to find happiness. He pursued Sheila far too quickly alas. Initially, the bohemian Malcolm charmed the elegant spinster. She admitted that he had "a lot more about him" than other men who she had met. However, after a few weeks she became standoffish

"Malcolm, I was around at my mother's house last weekend." She said, on the phone "They were clearing out the loft. There were these old newspapers from way back. There was a double spread on Julian Villette. Then in this Sunday's paper there was an article about you and those girls from Buzz-Whack. I'm afraid I can't see you any more. Just how many conquests have there been in the last twenty-five years?"

"The Lay-Off"

"You'll never play again son.... And you'll need a good long time in rehabilitation to even run on that again, I'm telling you."

I will never forget those heartbreaking words as the casualty doctor shook his head while tapping the illuminated x-ray. A few hours before then I was living in a different world entirely. I had a lifetime of soccer ahead of me. Then, all of a sudden I found myself that Saturday teatime pumped full of painkillers, everyone taking turns staring with screwed up noses at my swollen, sweating, mangled blackening knee. I had been stretchered off during a collision in the second half of a youth match. The doctor's words were an understatement to say the least. In the first couple of years after the injury, I had enough trouble even walking.

Soccer was my life. Soccer was my family. The sport meant everything to me. I had come right through the youth ranks of my local league club. They were very much *my* club. I had never wanted to play for anyone else. I had been out there on the terraces since the very first day my father carried me in on his shoulders. His father had carried him. As I grew up, I saw my club rise from non-league obscurity to League One. I grew to love everything about my club. It became an extended family. My whole weekly routine revolved around events at the club. Yet, more than just a fan, I could also play a little, thanks to tireless encouragement by my father. He was always very proud of my progress but never told me that. That was to be for my own good.

I got taken on as an apprentice youth player. I was a winger. I relied on short sharp bursts of pace. My speed was explosive. Yet, my first touch was poor and my second was barely satisfactory. But what I could do was knock it around a defender and beat him. And I could do it on anyone. Nobody had ever caught me one-on-one from a standing start. If a fullback had anything up to eight metres on me at the halfway line one-on-one, I'd skin him and make him look damned slow. Yet, I had little stamina and I couldn't run far. The manager said that if the 10 meters were an Olympic sport, I would have a gold medal. Of course the older pros had me sussed and read my runs but I was growing in stature and pace all the time. In one youth team match write-up, I was described as being a "continual threat" and another as a "nightmare dreaded by defenders"

I could also cross a good ball in. Albeit one-footed. My right foot could sweetly chip a ball onto a "coin from twenty five yards" according to another article in the local press. More than this, I also tended to "get stuck in" to a tackle and that always earned me a lot of respect. Yes, I had a decent career ahead of me. I was never going to be a big star and would probably never play in the Premier league but everyone was confident I could earn a respectable living in the lower leagues.

Looking back after the injury, it was frustrating and upsetting for me. I had so very nearly made it. I wasn't asking for a lot. If I could have only played in a first team shirt just once on one of those smoky winter nights I would have been satisfied. Just a minor cup match would have done but a League one match would have been perfect honour. I just wanted to represent my club at first-team level. Just once. I wanted my family and friends to see me win a match for the club.

After the injury, my father showed no signs of his disappointment, although inwardly he felt the same as me.

He was philosophical and put a positive spin on it. "Just forget it now son. Put it behind you. Find something else. Get a decent trade. Tradesmen earn a fortune. You are young enough. I wish I'd had your opportunities at your age."

The injury was back-page headlines in the local press for a couple of days afterwards. "Flying winger" and "Wing Commander" were some of the words used. The club had me insured for a small sum and looked after me for a short while. Things moved on and I became old news. A few matches are a long time in soccer. New heroes emerge and old ones are soon forgotten. The club continued without me, much to my disappointment. I didn't return to watch the club for ages afterwards.

Eventually, following the good advice from my parents, I trained to be an electrician and did quite well, considering. I was known for my limp. People did not remember me as the "promising winger who could have..." but rather as "that young lad who got a nasty injury". Yes, I did all right for myself in my new trade and made a decent living. In fact, I had probably done better than some of my fellow apprentices at the club.

It took me a long time to return to the terraces. It took me a longer time to learn to enjoy the matches once again.

My walking got easier eventually, without a stick. Occasionally, I tried to jog. My knee did not have enough movement to run.

One day some years later a session of idle Internet searching found an article about pioneering knee-ligament reconstructions that were beginning to be experimented with in Eastern Europe. These were designed to help extend the prospects of previously career-ending injuries of top athletes. It didn't take forever for me to make up my mind.

I used all my savings to fly to the former Russian state to have the operation. It was done in a week. Anyone and everyone had tried to talk me out of it. I didn't really want to listen.

Against all sorts of medical advice I signed away any chance of compensation or redress if the operation were to fail.

For weeks afterwards, and known only by myself, I was taking more painkillers than after the original injury.

Four months later my right knee was bending fully with the help of a private physiotherapist and four more weeks later I was kicking a ball again.

It wasn't long before 5-a-side games progressed into a few Sunday-league friendly matches. I kept out of the heavy tackles. I began to have a lot of contact with the club again. They were in all sorts of financial trouble languishing in the depths at the bottom of the league. They had nine first team players out with injuries and were having all sorts of problems even fielding a first eleven. All their allocation of loan players was used up, and they couldn't afford to bring any players in. The youth coach and several youth players were regularly turning out for the first team. Things were not looking good.

Under bizarre circumstances and mainly through past connections, pity and pestering, I turned up for training. At the age of 35, I was twice the age of some of my team -mates. I was spared most of the fitness drill; thank heaven. Mostly this was to do with my age but the first team coach had walked out when the manager was sacked. The chairman took the training sessions. He was desperate to leave to live abroad. The whole club's financial situation was in a right state. This gave me spirit to be even more passionate about saving my club.

"Non-contract basis mind, just week-to-week as emergency cover and you will have no insurance, you understand. Make sure you sign the registration papers in case we do have to call on you. If they deduct us any more points we'll never make up the ground. I must be nuts giving you a chance at your age but then I can remember you when you were a kid."

The money was of no interest. I would have paid them for the privilege to play. I was a real player and not a mercenary. That was what had ruined the club.

I was there in the dugout wrapped up warm. I had got there early before the game and mingled with the crowd. That excited me.

What else could you do on a dismal winter evening? The Damp, fog, floodlights, fag smoke, Bovril, pies, scarves. The beery smell of breath on the tough fans bizarrely dressed in just T-shirts as the sparse hard-core crowd trickled through the turnstiles. This was beautiful to me. We were all one big family. That was all I wanted. It was happiness. How could anyone not love to be involved with all this? And my name was written in the match programme with a squad number, and that meant everything to me and hopefully to my family. I was number 43. That indicated the turnover of players that season.

The club were by then down to their bare bones. By that midweek February fixture, they were really struggling for numbers and the chairman worried about fulfilling the fixture itself. The talk was about "winding up orders" and "liquidation." It didn't worry me, however.

"Listen. I won't use you unless I have to, but I know you can still clear a good ball without giving it away," The skipper told me in the warm up. "So I might need you in the second half. Some of these kids just aren't prepared to mix it when we've got our backs to the wall. If we don't get at least a point tonight, were knackered."

I came on just after half time. Our centre-half had concussion. I was told to play on the right of our back five. Well I would have even played in goal. My heart beat warmly. So that was what it actually felt like.

I had to do it. I bought the ball down in one. Our defence had pushed up quite far to catch them offside again, as was the game plan. I stayed back. Reading the bounce, I caught the ball sweetly dead centre of the studs under my right boot. The ball was tamed to a standstill as it tried to bounce thirty times in that second. It was sweet control and I heard some claps from the stand.

"Get rid!...bang it" the skipper screamed.

I could have done that.

I knocked it around the advancing midfielder to make him turn. We were then level but he had his back to the ball and that gave me at least two strides start. Taking a breath I took him on. You see I had to.

"No! Get bloody rid of it...!" I heard again.

Then I was past him. I knew he was not far behind. A few in the crowd began to shout. I wondered if any remembered me. My chest full, I pumped to keep the space between us. I knocked the ball further up the field in front of me.

There it was. As I accelerated, I could hear the sound of the wind against my ears. I remembered it from years ago. I pumped harder. No one could beat me. Nearly at my limit, my legs were less responsive and I felt my heart could burst at any moment. I could hear heavy steps only inches behind me pounding in the glue-pot of the pitch.

The noise of the crowd grew. Like sparks, suddenly there were two sharp pings.

Well, in the end I had made it. It was an ambition finally realised. That felt good if incomplete, but sometimes felt insignificant when measured against the words of the casualty doctor I saw that night.

"To be quite frank, son....*that* is a hell of a mess. Looking at your history and that dodgy surgery in there...I'm really not sure you'll walk again on that."

"My Tune"

For as long as I can remember, I had been a whistler. I think that it was only whistling that kept me happy. Perhaps I was a nervous whistler. It certainly kept me sane. When I wasn't whistling, I was humming. I did it constantly. It annoyed people and they were rude to me about it. I didn't give a toss, because it kept me happy.

When I was a little younger, I had been an obsessive record collector. I had literally thousands upon thousands of records, tapes in CDs in my collection. I was forever tripping over the things. They were everywhere. My house never needed to be vacuumed as there wasn't a square inch of floor not covered by a pile of them. To make things worse for those around me, I had an extensive knowledge of each and every one and its associated useless trivia. I must be very boring. This was probably one of the reasons I have never married.

People often asked me which was my favourite ever tune. It was also a question I often asked myself. With so very many to choose from, it was never an easy question to answer. However, after the events of one particular day, I could answer it without hesitation. I found a definite favourite. It was *the* tune. It was one tune that rose above all others. It was quite simply the ultimate piece of music. This tune made my neck hairs stand on end. This tune made me goose pimply and made me feel warm at the same time. The intervals between the notes were exactly the right intervals. It was just right. The problem was that I did not know what the tune was. I did not own a copy. I did not even know who wrote the tune. I must have whistled it a million times. I had hummed it and I had sung it. I had dreamed about it in my sleep. It was *my* tune. How many times had I heard the tune? I had heard it once and once only.

One summer morning, after taking the bus to work as usual, I had got off the stuffy bus two stops early to walk in the warmth. My walk took me past the park. It was a Saturday and the park was already beginning to fill with sunbathers. The weather was beautiful, people were relaxed and everyone was in a good mood. Some people had picnics and some had radios. We all have to make the most of our short and sweet summers.

As I walked past a group of lads I heard it. I actually was well past them when I realised exactly what I was listening to and I slowed down. I had to. I stopped and rested by the fence to listen to it. The group of lads were relaxing with their skateboards and taking a drink. One of them had some sort of radio or cassette player with them and the tune was coming from there for certain. I tried to listen more carefully. What was this clever tune? I was struggling at this point because of the other background noises in the park.

This tune was perfect. It was haunting. I just had to find out what it was. It took the form of a kind of simple piano instrumental but I could not pick out any more details and it could have been a part of some longer piece. There may have been a vocal over the top but I could not pick it out. I had to get closer. I wandered nearer to the lads. At first they ignored me. One nudged another and then two of them began to stare at me menacingly and suspiciously. I knew this was going to happen. They frowned at me. I tried to get closer, just to listen to the tune. I wanted to hear the announcer name who the song was by. Then I could get on with the job of getting hold of a copy. That was all I wanted. I needed to own this song. I wanted to buy it that very day.

"What do you want?" Asked the first to catch my eye, scowling in that way that only teenage lads can do properly. They seemed to scowl at everything at that age.

"What are you after?"

"Don't talk. I'm listening." I thought. "Shut up"

I tried to smile without looking directly at them.

I did not answer as I was concentrating on listening intently.

"Oi you... I'm talking to you mister."

I had to answer. "Er…, I'm just listening to the radio lads. What tune is that playing?"

"You what?..........What you want?"

"Just shut up, I'm going to miss it." I thought to myself.

They all stood up and tried to look defensive. One of them knocked over the radio as he got up. I think it moved it out of tune. Only static came out of the radio. The tune was lost.

"I'm just trying to hear that music on the radio lads".

They came quite close and squared up to me.

"Any idea what song that was lads? Have you heard it before at all?"

"You better get lost or we'll av ya" was their reply.

They became more aggressive and started to push me away.

"What channel was it on lads?"

I was pushed to the ground. Things were going to get nasty. I had to retreat. I was angry and upset. I walked away sweating and totally frustrated. I wracked my brain. I tried to remember the tune. I went back to the lads later sneaking up on them to see if I could at least recognise the radio channel. Perhaps I could have phoned the radio station. They were busy with their skateboarding. The radio was still lying down where they knocked it over earlier. I left sadly.

I tried to hum the tune to colleagues. I went into countless record shops and whistled the tune to many bewildered staff. I tried a lot of stores soon after that day but when I had exhausted all those I still kept trying whenever I was in a different town.

This literally went on for years.

One Saturday, In London, while shopping and probably while humming, I met my old college girlfriend shopping in a department store. It was a complete shock as it had been many years since I saw her last.

She was actually my only serious girlfriend. We had a lot to talk about. I barely recognised her. She had obviously done well for herself. She was expensively dressed and stank of money.

I mentioned over coffee in a restaurant afterwards that she seemed to have done very well for herself. She explained that her wealth had come from Mike. Mike was her son. Mike had been hugely successful for a short period of time some years before. Mike was a musician. One thing she had never told me when we split up from one-another was that she was pregnant. Mike was in fact my son. She had always meant to tell me but had somehow never got round to it. She felt that she didn't need me. We had lost contact years ago and anyway there was apparently no way of tracing me.

It was a lot for me to take in. It was all of a sudden, a big day for me. I was a father. I had always wanted to be a father. I had been a father for thirty years apparently and had never known a thing about it. I was, belatedly, a proud father.

At the weekend I got hold of one of Mike's CDs. The tune was track three.

Steve Morris

"Older not Wiser"

Twenty years. Twenty years had gone by before we actually counted them. It was amazing just how quickly the time had passed considering that he was literally stuck in his bedroom for most of the period. We all blamed satellite TV, computers, Internet shopping and games consoles for making it all too easy. We all blamed failures by the health system, the waiting lists, under-funding and an ability of a patient to literally slip through the system un-noticed for year after year. I could get into the politics of it but that did not matter now.

He was cured. Timothy was Timothy again.

He was 17 when he first broke down with severe anxiety and depression. Tim became very withdrawn. This then developed over time into agoraphobia. He refused to leave the upstairs of his house. The actual cause was never fully understood. Who cared exactly what had caused it? He was cured now.

By the time of his recovery, he was around 37. He was still a young man. He had plenty of time left and was ready to face the world again.

A chance treatment by a new antidepressant, labelled by the press "The confidence drug", had done the trick. This was helped by a lovely warm spell of early spring weather. It was a miracle cure really. Within six weeks of starting the treatment, he was out and about. His parents both cried the first few times he went out on his own.

The time was for a fresh start for everyone concerned.

With everyone ready for a new beginning, they moved home to live by the sea. A family holiday was also promptly booked. They all agreed to forget the last twenty years and to start a new life.

Not that things were going to be easy for Timothy. He was very naïve in the outside world. Far from being streetwise, he looked, acted and thought clumsily, like a kid. In many ways it looked as if he had barely aged at all. We all assumed that this was due to the lack of pollutants, alcohol, cigarettes, late nights and Tim's obsessively healthy diet that had all contributed to his remarkably youthful appearance.

His mother suggested that he join the local Church social group in order to meet people again. Timothy agreed.

He started off quite well and, giving only a limited amount of information about his background, he was taken under the wing of a young couple called Alison and Peter who ran the youth group.

They took him on the usual group-type outings with the other "young" people to ten-pin bowling nights, meals and to cinemas.

His first tentative steps into the real social world were quite difficult and needed far more effort than the quick walks around the park that he started out with.

The world had changed a lot. Fashions, music, shops, prices and methods of payment were all different. Everybody had a mobile phone glued to an ear. Even the way people spoke seemed entirely different than the way he remembered from two decades before. Although he had watched a lot of TV, Tim sighed as he realised he had a lot to re-learn.

He was impressed that there was far less cigarette smoke around than there used to be. It all bought back nice memories of the days before his breakdown when, for a brief but magical period, evenings out were an exciting time. Perhaps they were remembered in such a precious way because they were so very brief. It was like the memories we all get of our favourite childhood holidays. He fondly remembered his then teenage girlfriend Jilly and wondered what falling in love now would feel like.

Conveniently, he never got around to telling Alison and Peter his true age and, as they never asked, he avoided divulging that information. They were wonderful people with only the best of intentions. They wouldn't have excluded him from activities but Timothy was enjoying being "looked after". Life was good.

A routine visit to the local GP was necessary to continue with the prescription of the anti-depressant drug. Tim told him the entire story. The GP was particularly pleased that the drug had such a positive effect and he was keen for Timothy to continue with it. The doctor found accounts of Tim's new lease of life quite amusing and jokingly said that Tim should pretend he was actually a teenager and take advantage of the situation.

Tim tried to dress in the current teenage fashions as best he could. Peter from the youth group assumed that Tim was just another isolated teenager lacking in confidence and social skills. The youth club was an opportunity for these types of young people to integrate into a more wholesome social scene with a Christian ethos in the background. Tim had a couple of close calls when he nearly gave the game away but somehow managed to keep up his "white lie". Peter, a trendy young man of ironically the same age as Tim suggested that Tim might bring his image up-to-date. The two "men" went shopping for new clothes and Tim went as far as getting his ears pierced and hair bleached.

Twenty years ago his mother would have gone mad. Arriving home this time after his belated makeover, his mother greeted him with a tearful hug. Even a temporary tattoo did not faze his parents.

Spring flowed nicely into summer and Timothy grew in confidence. He was on a high. The family made plans for him to attend college so as to set a direction for some sort of career. Needless to say, Tim lied about his age on the application form. He was offered a place.

He continued to be increasingly attached to the Church group. He enjoyed the novelty of the social life. He was not put under any pressure and lived his life for the evenings out. Tim had also quickly become very attracted to a member of the social group called Polly.

Polly was exceptionally pretty. She was warm and bubbly but not confident. Polly had an infectious smile and was one of those girls who always seemed to be blushing.

He hoped that this was a good sign for him. Whenever Tim closed his eyes, Tim saw Polly's face. He quite simply could not get her out of his head. Not that he wanted to. If he could not sleep, he thought of Polly. He was quite happy about that. It was love.

It was ironic that whenever his parents suggested that he should do something he did not agree with his reply was always that he was "not a kid" and "was a mature adult". When they suggested that he should spend more time planning for his future and less time with the group, the reverse applied.

The eighteen-year-old Polly thought Tim a little serious at first. He was always a little nervous around her, for some reason. However, she was impressed with his clean living lifestyle.

Gradually, the mutual attraction developed. Although a little clumsy with social skills, Tim had wider general knowledge far beyond other boys his age. To her, she felt secure in the company of a boy who seemed to have read everything. Several times with Polly, he almost let things slip when commenting on his love of songs released years ago.

The first night they went out together, his parents despaired of the fact that he did not return until 2:00 AM. The real truth was that after dutifully walking Polly home at 10:00 PM, Tim had walked round and round the town. The smell of her perfume lingered on his coat on a night that he wanted to last forever. Well, it was a night that was twenty years overdue. Life was great.

Tim and Polly enjoyed the rest of the summer holiday, spending as much time together as they could. With little else to occupy his mind, Tim would often count the hours until the next date with Polly. She was going to college in the autumn and Tim was happy to be going to the same place of learning.

This satisfied his parents, who, largely unaware of the exact details of Tim's new friends and the extent of his "white lies", were happy that he was planning for the future. Everyone was happy.

A week into term, Tim and Polly had been to a local funfair on the Friday night. The lights and sounds combined with the smell of candyfloss and the clingingly overcooked hot-dog onions worked deep into the heart of Tim. Later, when he walked her back to her home, Polly invited Tim in for a coffee where he would get a chance to say "Hello" to her extended family for the first time. Polly's family were many. As well as her parents, her two younger brothers busied themselves at a noisy computer game, much to the annoyance of Polly's two aunts. Reluctantly, the nervous fraudster Tim fidgeted into the cosy room and he sat on the sofa opposite Polly's many people.

He began to feel stressed.

"Nice to…..er, hang on a minute. I know you…Timothy Richards!" said one of the women called Jilly.

"If I could Bottle it"

"Oooh.... That really took me back." I overheard him say.

"Did you smell that then? I've not smelled that for years. Wow. I remember it now. .....Hey, remember Eddie's shirts? Hey, can...." and so he went on.

The first time I heard those words I was working on the top floor of our department store. With little else to do, and trying to look busy, I was doing some people-watching of the shoppers passing by the perfume counter opposite where I was supposed to be merchandising our new shirts. It was the same story all that day. It fascinated me how their heads just picked up and reacted the very moment they first caught a sniff of the retro 1970s aftershave. The fuss was caused by small samples of a "limited-edition" free gift bottle given away with a new aftershave range. It was meant to smell similar to some long-gone 1970s favourite. I saw those first shoppers later that day on another floor of the store. They still seemed to be smiling, to be reminiscing and they had many bags under their arms. They were having a good day.

I actually decided to do something clever about this when I saw a similar thing happening again the next day. I had set up a gift display stall near a food counter where they were giving out samples of some new range of healthy wheat crackers. Samples of various spreads were available to try with the crackers. Instead of spreading a thin layer of his choice of jam or marmalade over a cracker, one guy took a jar from the back, wrapped a large swirl of rich brown malt around his white plastic spoon and swallowed with his eyes closed. Again I heard the words "Ah... That took me right back." And then smiling he went on, "My grandmother used to make me have that. I hated it then! But now it tastes great. I remember when...." Then he went on about childhood reminiscences much to the annoyance of his friends no doubt for the rest of the shopping trip and probably, I could imagine, all the way home.

I was on to something here.

Sometimes, no matter just how bad those long-gone days actually had been at the time, in hindsight we always seem to feel the same warm nostalgia when looking back. It puts us into a dreamy mood. We become glossy-eyed and travel elsewhere for a brief moment or two in time. Forgotten scents seem to bring our memories back like no other sense. It was amazing just what memories some smells could actually resurrect. I decided that for once in my life at least, I had a damned good idea that would work. This one was a killer.

What I intended to do was to quite literally re-release a few "long-gone" scents and smells into the noses of the credit-card-carrying punter. I aimed to make people briefly remember the very best moments of their lives, feel good about themselves and then spend more. Simple really. Everyone is a winner.

I knew I wasn't the first to spot this tactic. Our baker on the ground floor had for a few years regularly pumped the smell of freshly baked bread back into the store, although it was always denied. I was sure our in-store café did the same thing with their fresh coffee. We all soon felt hungry even if we only came in for a bar of soap. It worked every time.

Christmas was to be the key. That was usually the happiest of times. We all look fondly back to our childhood Christmas memories. I had to find some long-gone Christmas smells. Not the obvious ones, however, such as trifles and turkey. We still had those smells to this day. They hadn't changed a lot. Anyone could recreate those without much trouble. I needed to think about which age group had the spending power at the moment. Then I had to look at what period they would have been young and particularly enjoying Christmas. Then I had to accurately research the sort of things that were hanging around the Christmas tree at that particular time. If I could waft that around their noses, they might get quite nostalgic and feel like a spend-up. I know that I would.

I first thought that the development of the "dog nose" technology couldn't have come at a better time for me. Basically it is a kind of smell "amplifier". The device went on sale coincidentally around the time I had my idea. We all know that a dog has nose sensitivity around fifty times that of ours. This nasal implant allowed the wearer to have greatly enhanced abilities of smell. I did try one as part of my research. I could see that it had its use in forensic sciences and in criminal detection but I can see why it did not take off as a lifestyle accessory. Some smells, you just don't want to smell any more strongly than they already are.

The implant was quickly inserted into my nostrils under local anaesthetic. I went outside into the high street. Tobacco smoke blew into my face from a hundred meters away. Perfumes and after shaves from people in the street wafted competitively with their body odours towards me with every draught. I could smell the breath of people before I could make out their faces. Cocaine was obviously present on many people's clothes as I mingled with shoppers. The drains turned my stomach. Curry houses choked me. It really was bizarre. Were animals really subject to this every day? I decided then to go for quality not quantity when I manufactured my scents. I wanted to make people feel happy not nauseous. Over-powering scents just would not have the right outcome. The implant was duly removed by my request and my research returned to developing my seventies time warp.

With help from some of my housemates who were at the time studying chemistry at university, I read into the plastics and metals that were used to make tinsels and those kitsch artificial Christmas trees of the time. I looked at the tacky useless gifts that were found in crackers and the coloured dyes used in those paper hats so thin they used to rip on the smallest of heads. I looked at the additives in the chocolate on those silver-paper wrapped ornaments that hung from the tree. It was amazing how they didn't melt next to those fairy lights. Heaven knows what was in them. Maybe that was why our generation of kids were the first to grow out of control as they reached their teens.

I persuaded the broke university post-graduates to research ways of re-creating these very special smells of specially selected plastics and metals used in Christmas decorations in the 1970s. They put together a list and some other chemistry students began to manufacture samples from which to produce some fumes. It took a little mixing to make it appealing rather than just being over-powering. They looked at tinsel, streamers, candles and the toys of the time. Fortunately a lot of those toys were readily available via collectors. One clever brainbox stayed up all night for a few quid just to isolate the magic ingredient that gave a certain extinct early-70s soap smell its characteristic perfume. "I haven't smelled that one for forty years!" someone exclaimed later.

The "Sea-Air" one was a cynically deadly idea. Oh, I was proud of that one. Next to Christmas time, our favourite memories as kids are usually of trips to the seaside. Just thinking about it now, and closing my eyes, I can still feel the warmth in my belly. In the seventies, for many people, these were still taken in the UK. We worked hard on capturing the smells of those smiley sunny days. We looked back for the original recipes for candyfloss, popcorn, sweets, hot dogs, tobacco smoke and most crucially, those ingredients of that supposedly fresh seafood that was always available in cartons on the piers. You could smell it literally from streets away. Fantastic. I swear they even managed to work into the formula, a little of that almost-foul stagnant water that lay forever in rock pools and under the piers. They managed to concentrate it with a propellant so it could work in a spray can. I got quite emotional the first time I got a sniff of the finished formula. This idea did it for me far more than the Christmas formula. I was away for at least twenty minutes when I got a waft of the "Sea air". First, I felt the warmth in my chest. Then, it was amazing how one memory led to another and a trail was set to something forgotten years ago. The science students had done a very clever cash-in-hand job for me with the mixtures, although ironically none of them were actually old enough to fully appreciate them.

I knew that it would clearly work. It would have to be used separately from the Xmas potion, however. Mixing them together just wouldn't do.

It was quite expensive to produce in the end. We needed to test each and every can individually by a human. It was impossible to program a computer to test how good a retro scent smelled! It was a time consuming process. Each aerosol formula can was, for some technical reason, uniquely different. Each can had its own unique signature so some cans actually worked better than others. The health and safety people began to watch us closely.

The first place it was used in anger was at a large music festival. I sold some cans to the promoter at a bargain price, as it was so far untested commercially. People reacted very well. Tears were soon bought to people's eyes and lumps to their throats without them realising the reasons why. The concert was quite subdued at the beginning and there was a lot of hugging but people were certainly up-for-it as the show got going.

People had bought their tickets before the event so it was difficult to measure the effect on consumer spending. We needed to know about pounds and pence.

After quickly patenting the product I offered it first of all, due to loyalty, to our department store owners. It certainly worked. Reports slowly began to emerge in the press. Instead of being cynical about it, the general public accepted that this sales tactic may be used on them and most actively sought out places where it was rumoured to be used.

Timing was everything. I had a word with the person who chose the CDs for the piped shopping music in our store. I realised that memories could be linked to the "sounds of the day".

I made big money for the first time in my life. I became a different person from the one who earned a pittance on the long dull days on the top floor of the store. It had been on sale for nearly two years when the call first came.

Ironically it was from the same University where we had worked on the formula. Their medical faculty specialising in cancer research had been watching our progress closely.

They informed me that I should engage a defence lawyer urgently.

"All around us"

Thinking back, it *was* an ideal morning for it. Indian summer had snatched a lovely rich crisp Saturday morning from cloak of the oncoming autumn. We had the whole of winter ahead of us so we intended to make the most of any valuable days like that. The weather was still pleasantly mild. Lack of any breeze meant that we climbed through some early morning mist that was just beginning to clear. The local farmers had not yet started chugging their tractors around the fields below and there was little traffic noise to be heard anywhere. It was great. We felt superior to the rooks circling around below. We could have been back in time a full thousand years. At any moment I expected some distinguished knight of the Middle Ages to casually saunter around the corner.

We loved our walks up to Beeston Castle on Saturday mornings. The dogs loved it even more. Standing majestically on the top of one of Cheshire's few hills, on a clear day it has some superb views in all directions. Looking across to a neighbouring misty hillside castle, we were always impressed that, for a moment or two anyway, we saw the world exactly as it was seen a millennium earlier. Brilliant.

I almost forgot to try out the camera. I took some shots of the dogs, the misty landscape views and even my wife Janine in that particular order. I wanted to try out a new camera lens I'd recently made so I finished off the entire roll of film. Afterwards, I put the camera back in my coat, and then we walked back down the hill and, as far as I can remember, drove away to Tarporley for our usual Saturday shopping ritual. I remember that it was a good day, but I can't remember anything remarkable about it.

The actual 'fun and games' began a month or so later when I developed the photographic film of that day together with a load of other ones in my darkroom.

I worked as an industrial research chemist involved in glass and optics development. Also, I was a semi-professional photographer, hence the obsession. I had been working on developing some new types of camera lenses. This particular slightly green lens involved the use of a so-far untried type of silica. The silica in question was ground out of some opals that had been in a colleague's attic for years. The stones were possibly African in origin but were apparently not particularly valuable in terms of monetary value. It was his idea to grind them into glass. Over the years I had tried all sorts of mixtures, temperatures and processes with the aim of producing special-effect camera lenses. Then, with the onset of digital photography, I was beginning to feel that I had missed my chance. I was determined to try anything to make the perfect lens.

At first I assumed I had actually developed the wrong film or that some other film had got mixed up with one of mine. I distinctly remember that Janine and I were up there at the castle alone that morning. So who were all the people in the photos? It was complete mayhem. There were people everywhere. It was like a packed tube train and as if no one could move. Bizarrely, I could see that some of the figures were super-imposed over other ones. I also noticed that the figures did not have sharp outlines compared with the body of Janine, who was in the centre of each photo. One figure was partly in front of her! Two films had obviously been merged together. I closely examined the negatives.

I actually rang Janine at work to tell her and that evening she had a good look at the photos.

"There must have been something already on that film" she suggested.

I assured her that we photographers used only the best quality film. Then things became more interesting.

"Look at their clothes…how fascinating" said Janine. Now I hadn't picked up on this. Ever observant, Janine had noticed that the people's clothes were quite significant. It was like a scene from some television costume drama. Although varied in styles, drab, dirty and roughly sewn, their clothes seemed genuinely primitive, even mediaeval. I also noticed how dirty the visible patches of skin seemed on some of the people. Facial skin seemed visible only on the women. Beneath dented rusting helmets it seemed that all the men were covered in dark matted facial hair. Facial expressions did not fit in with some student charity fancy-dress event, and I again began to wonder where the source of the film had originated. It was not one of mine for sure. The figures did not look as if the costume department of some film company had dressed them nor did they look particularly happy. They actually looked like the real thing.

With no conclusion, we went back downstairs and switched on the TV. Mogridge, the TV "celebrity medium" was on that night again. He always seemed to be on. I disliked him but Janine insisted on watching his show because he always "seemed to get it right". The cantankerous old alcoholic was raking it in. He was charging people to visit their homes and answer questions about their unsolved family mysteries. I hated the way he always wore that black pullover, his old wrinkled face squinting through that ridiculous monocle. That night Mogridge told a bewildered family where some deceased aunt had hidden her jewels in their house.

"Set up for sure." I thought to myself.

"Try the camera lens out again." The ever-logical Janine suggested over breakfast.

I did. This time I used it on another camera. I took it out with me during the day and fired off the film in various lights and locations to see how it performed. Later, when I initially developed the second film, I felt relieved. The photos I took were of our garden, the woods and a few of the dogs when I took them out later on that day. I was relieved that there were no more images of crowds of people and I left the photos on the kitchen table. So I got on with the rest of my day.

"Who's that guy in the garden?" Asked Janine that night.

Instinctively I looked out of the kitchen window.

"No! I mean on the photo. Look there's a man standing on the back left hand corner of the lawn. Who's he?"

I looked more closely. Like before, I had missed this. He was a little hazy and a little transparent, but he was there for certain. A male figure was in the photo wearing a greyish brown tight-fitting suit with elbow patches. Eerily, he seemed to be looking straight at me. But if he was there when I took the photo, why hadn't I seen him at the time?

We looked at each other. We examined the other photos. They were mostly sharp except for the one I took of the dogs near to the woods. There was distinctly a group of figures crossing the path of the dogs in the distance. A little blurred in appearance, I cannot accurately describe their clothes but there were four or five people huddled together, heads down, walking into the wood. Again, I was adamant that there was no one there when I took that photo. Now, our dogs are particularly boisterous and always jump up at strangers. Sneaking past a dog unnoticed is not easy. So there was my proof. The dogs had not seen them either.

Suddenly Janine tapped her finger frantically on the photo.

"Ghosts, Mike………..They're ghosts!" Janine exclaimed without even looking up.

And we knew they were. There was nothing else they could be.

I was cold. I was hot. I was excited, terrified, goose-pimpled, emotional and sweating. That was how I felt that evening. There was no sleep for me or for either of us for a while then. We sat up all that night, phoned in sick in the morning and sat up the next few nights.

I removed the lens from the camera. For reasons I am sure you can appreciate, I placed it to my eye during the daylight hours only. I scanned the garden and the woods beyond. By mid-morning I had seen our little huddled group of "friends" walk past again. I said, "walk" where I really meant, "drift" as they did not have any visible feet. There weren't many ghosts around to be honest. That came as a relief. At least there weren't many in our immediate street.

Janine persuaded me to go into town with the lens to have a look. I peeped out of the safety of my car window, peering gingerly through my green tinged lens. There they were. There were hundreds of them all over the place. They were crossing the road. They were drifting in and out of doorways. I could tell that they were often angry, frustrated and yelling at one-another. There was no sound from any of them, despite their screams. It was interesting to watch a bunch of grubby old miners in helmets walking alongside a blissfully unaware girl with a pram. By definition, ghosts are the unsettled spirits, so this would explain why there were not literally millions of them everywhere. The "settled" ghosts would be spending their time elsewhere, I assumed.

So there it was. By pure chance, I had made a lens that allowed the viewer to see ghosts. It was as simple as that. I had no idea of how it worked. Ghosts, it seems, have been all around us, sharing our world day and night without us ever knowing. As well as being so obviously scary, however, it was quite upsetting. Some of the ghosts were very disturbing to see and often had met obviously very traumatic ends. In just three days, it had changed the way my wife and I looked at the world quite literally. I just couldn't believe I was actually viewing them with my own eyes. It was very alarming. We lived in constant dread of seeing some ghost from our own families pay us a visit, and thanked our good luck that we had not lived in our present home for long. We soon decided that we were better off before we could see them.

"If we destroyed the lens, do you think we could forget all about what we've seen?"

We both thought about it. Mogridge was on the TV again. His show took on a whole new meaning. I looked at the TV screen through the lens but I saw no ghosts via the picture, even on Mogridge's show.

"I don't think we could ever forget." I replied after some thought. Some things in life can never be forgotten.

"These lenses could make people pretty freaked out if they went on sale. Would you buy one for your favourite nephew?" Janine said. "The world would not be a happier place. That's for sure. What the eye doesn't see, if you know what I mean. Bin it."

I smashed it and threw it in the garbage. I burned the photos and the negatives.

Let someone else discover them, hopefully when I'm long dead and gone.

Looking at Mogridge recently again on TV, I understood how he did it. Now it was exactly obvious to me what the miserable old medium had stuck in his eye all these years. Someone else had by accident come across the optical properties of these gemstones years ago. Mogridge didn't have a gift to talk to spirits. He *was* a rogue after all but I wasn't going to tell anyone. Nor was he. Some things are better left how they are.

Steve Morris

"Life's too short"

"Sleeping is *my* biggest waste of time. I mean.... we spend one third of our lives doing it. Why? Do we really need to sleep *every* night? Life is getting so busy these days; I just can't really fit in the time for sleep." Darren Rogers told his private consultant.

"And I always take a power nap when the Asian markets close in the afternoons. Things go a bit quieter then." the stockbroker went on while the doctor filled out the prescription. Admittedly, Darren did occasionally take the odd nap. This was not very often though. At that time, he had got so over-tired and irritable by the time Fridays came around that he wasn't able to get any sleep over the weekend when he actually got the chance to.

Scientists working on a "problem" faced by astronauts, had by then found a way of switching off the biological mechanism that made people fall asleep. Mother Nature has a way of telling our bodies that after a day's hunting and gathering, our batteries need recharging. Triggered by our body clock, signals are sent to the brain to make us feel sleepy. A drug had been developed for the astronauts to temporarily block these pathways, so they could maximise the use of their time in space. Darren had read all about this.

Within a few days of taking the drug, patients reported leaving their former sleep patterns behind. Although expensive and difficult to obtain, the designer drug became the ultimate lifestyle accessory to the most competitive of stockbrokers. They were keen to play all of the world's stock markets without wasting their time and talents by fruitlessly sleeping through one third of their potential opportunities to make a killing.

Ironically, they were one of only a few types of people who could afford the private treatment.

At any given hour in the world there was always a market in operation.

We were living in a twenty-four hour digital world market and the best players of the world's markets simply couldn't afford to miss a single hour of it. The driven Darren often put the odd twenty-fifth hour in. He knew that a lot could be won and lost in an hour, let alone during an entire night's sleep. He worked out in his head how much sleeping at night was actually costing him in lost commissions.

It was a drug that had been designed for short-term use only. Apparently, it had worked fine on the rats and monkeys with hardly any side effects. Darren noticed that new drugs always seemed to be that way. That only meant that they hadn't been properly trialled in the long-term before they went on general release. Well, Darren only needed help for a few months, to see him through until he'd earned enough commission for that French property they had set their mind on.

The consultant explained to Darren that some rest was important, as was quality time with his wife and friends. The go-getting stockbroker was fully aware that there had always been high doses of caffeine and stimulant medications to keep people going during busy periods, or when "cramming" for exams. However, after a few nights "on the go", fatigue always caught up with people in the end and they were useless for days afterwards. Bingeing on stimulants was acceptable once-in-a-while but he needed a sustained fix.

After a couple of very near misses over the last year, and much to the relief of his wife, Darren had given up driving home from work. He could no longer guarantee staying awake at the wheel. Even that obsessed workaholic didn't see what use the chateau would be to him if he were in an early grave.

"Look, this is just until the new year," He told Julie, his patient wife.

She explained how her law career had blossomed without the need for artificial stimulants.

He was surprised to find that the pills didn't give him a "high". Instead, they seemed only to slow him down a little, and to keep his general alertness on a constant level rather than have peaks and troughs to his hour-by-hour energy levels.

The private prescription was expensive and he kept his secret between himself and his wife, Julie. He wanted to steal a lead on his competitors. Such was his trade.

"If you want a level playing field, you are playing the wrong game." He often said out of earshot.

After simply feeling a little strange for a few days, he worked for the first time right through a weekday night. Darren was actually so busy that first night he kept forgetting to check the time anyway. He allowed himself a feeling of achievement early next morning, when he squinted at the sun prising its way through the cracks in his office curtains. He had felt admittedly sleepy but didn't actually nod off all the way through that night. Darren was pleased. After a few more days he was surviving on an hour's sleep in any twenty-four hour period and by the following week even less sleep than that.

Darren had been clearly warned by the consultant to avoid any strenuous exercise, recreational drugs, alcohol and caffeine in order for the drug to work properly. To him, that was perfectly reasonable but when the time came "out of the blue" of the unprecedented global economic stock market crash and its subsequent recovery, there was big money to be made for the early-bird trader. To be in with his best chance he had to stay within sight of four PCs and three telephones continuously for about 72 hours without a break. His wife kept him fed and watered at his desk. Cordless phones were taken in and out the adjoining bathroom. When the market turmoil was all over and even Darren was fully satisfied of that fact, he did not collapse in a heap. Instead he took a shower, had more breakfast then began work as normal by spending a day ringing around his regular clients. He was glad that in this digital age, he did not have to travel between clients. That would have been a sheer waste of time, and for Darren, "Life was just too short" for that.

His wife complained about the colour of his eyes. He actually took a short nap in the back of a taxi while journeying back to see the private hospital consultant. Darren left his phone on "vibrate" just in case.

Darren had changed. The odd short naps he got were littered with vividly surreal dreams. Moods became unpredictable, but he never became overly excited or withdrawn. Occasionally he would have bouts of memory loss and headaches. Occasionally Julie heard him running around the grounds of the Chateau screaming albeit as quietly as he could. His hair receded, and he developed prostate problems. Myopia followed.

"You look more like 50 than thirty Darren. We need a holiday." She often said.

His consultant was satisfied with Darren's general condition but was reluctant to re-issue too much more of the prescription.

The stockbroker soon found out that one of his friends had got hold of a similar prescription and then heard of another doing the same. Soon, as word got around, quite a number of his wealthy colleagues confessed to hoping to try the drug and some articles in the media soon appeared. Darren soon despaired that it was ironic that if all brokers could stay awake for twenty-four hours in every day then he would have to remain permanently on the drug and find another way of stealing a lead on his competitors.

Darren had originally planned to make his first million by the time he was thirty. That milestone was to arrive well ahead of schedule. Even before taking the medication he was well past the "one million bucks" mark and after six months of working nocturnally, he was well past several millions. Julie and Darren had reached an agreement that, as part of their plan, they would aim for their first child that year. Like many modern people, Darren had never even considered, let alone doubted his own fertility until he had actually tried to make a baby. A series of IVF treatment failures bought the specialist conception consultant to almost give up on a man with such very little potential of fertility. Advising Darren to relax and take a long holiday was rather pointless. At that point Darren remembered Julie just turning to stare blankly out of the window of the consulting room.

The baby never came but the ambitious couple did buy their dream home as part of their plan. However, somehow life at the chateau was a little incomplete. Darren, rather than continue with their original plan to slowly wind-down for early retirement, took on more work than ever. He had tried, at Julie's request, to taper off the use of his medication but found the daytimes foggy and cloudy and felt hung over if he managed to "get his head down" the previous night. He had severe withdrawal symptoms and at times, he was so agitated he couldn't even sit down. Smoking and drinking did not relieve the tension. Therefore he resumed the drug. Julie often found that although she had eventually persuaded him to let up on the work a little, she found that her husband was addicted to computer games and online gambling throughout the small hours.

This went on for ten years. Ten long years went very quickly. Julie felt that she had had enough. She finally gave him an ultimatum and much to his credit, he chose her over the drug. Work was finished. They had money. They had no family. Darren was pretty useless.

The couple were to have only a brief retirement.

Julie sat in front of the coroner with many questions.

"But he was only 46, doctor. He still had a third of his life left at least."

"Natural causes, Julie...Natural causes just like those other two brokers. I've seen about twenty of them so far this year. Who originally prescribed him that stuff to stop him sleeping? Three score years and ten? Well.... you do the maths."

"Shared House"

"It's about time you settled down and built one for yourself".

Just about everyone had been saying that to me for the last few years. So I eventually succumbed to the pressure. It *was* about time indeed. They were right. I had been putting it off.

I was an architect and builder. I had been very successful in my work and I slept well at night knowing that I had made many other people happy over the years. I knew my business well. Yet, like those gifted hairdressers to the stars who always seem to have unkempt hair themselves, my family and I lived in a rather ordinary home in need of some major repairs. With the success of the business came early retirement and so the opportunity to build something extra-special for us.

I had designed bespoke property developments for wealthy clients all over Europe. My opinions were widely respected and I had even been persuaded to appear on some of those many television property shows that I usually detested.

Our new home, we decided, was to be the very best I could build. After extensive research, we managed to buy an idyllic plot of land in the Scottish Highlands and fortunately obtained the necessary planning permission without any problems.

I soon set about working on the design from our comparatively ugly house in the city. As soon as I had made the decision to start the project, I was counting the days until we could move in. I now had the time to source the very best in building materials from all over Europe and even beyond. I had built up countless contacts over the years. Although it was a "new build" property, we decided that our bespoke house would contain lots of genuine original period features from some of our favourite tastes. We wanted the house to look classically old without looking contrived or tacky. There was to be no Mock-Tudor or bolted-on ceiling beams in our house. In fact, there was to be no "mock" anything in our house. If we wanted it, we would have it and it would be the genuine article.

I got hold of lots of Scottish sandstone from a row of ancient cottages that were beyond repair. The floor tiles were from a very special old Spanish property. Their colour was improving with age. We used some beautiful Welsh slate on the roof and some of the huge timber beams were German. They were a lovely natural mahogany colour and they would be visible right through our open-plan living room. The paving slabs that were to form our huge patio were of a unique stone from India. The shipping cost was not cheap.

We had only been in our house four weeks before things literally started to go "bump". We began to hear strange noises at night.

Yes, we knew instantly what they were. At first it was only simple shuffling and scraping in the small hours. However, things developed, and we saw the momentary characteristic blue-and-green glows out of the corners of our eyes. They always seemed to be gone when we looked their way. It was a good job that the kids had left for university. They would not have put up with it. Next, we started to hear whispers in the night. The whispers gradually developed into voices. The voices were not the characteristic low moaning ones usually attributable to spirits. They were agitated, bickering, almost arguing voices that bantered to and fro from different parts of the house. Obviously the place was deeply haunted. Of this there was absolutely no doubt. We had to get this sorted out; otherwise it would be an end of my happy retirement and good sleeping habits.

"This is a new house. It had only been up for four weeks. Just how on Earth can the place be haunted?" Asked my wife Pat.

We had chosen the location carefully. I was pretty thorough in my research of the plot of land. I had found that the field had never before been built on other than having a winter barn. There was no record of any history there at all really, let alone graveyards or battlefields anywhere near.

The noises got louder and more annoying. A further development was that they would occasionally break out during the day.

Pat went to stay with her mother for a few days. I think it was the constant door slamming while she was showering upstairs on the Friday, which was the last straw for her. One had even broken a pane of Italian stained glass in the kitchen door. Something had to be done. Pat left insisting that things were "sorted out" before she returned.

I'm not a religious man and knew nothing about this kind of thing. However, I did call in the local priest.

It was much like those situations where your car dashboard warning lights flash madly all day long until the very moment when you drive into the garage. Like the faulty electronic components that suddenly right themselves, those mischievous spirits went silent for an hour or two while the priest was there. He reluctantly blessed the house and invited us to church. I feel he did not take me seriously at all.

They started up again in earnest that night. I heard distinct voices this time but I could not make out what they were saying. This time things were beginning to get thrown around. When I woke the next day, the jardinière was over and some plates had been sent across the kitchen.

This was going on and on. I phoned Pat to explain. She insisted on staying away until "the buggers were all out".

At this time the patio was eventually being laid. The delayed flags had come from India. It seemed that as soon as that process began, utter ghostly chaos started at night. That night there were the usual whispers, then voices, shouting and the slamming of doors. However, this time, before midnight there were what seemed like hundreds of voices all simultaneously yelling at one-another. I picked out some words and they seemed foreign to me. I'd had enough. I checked into a nearby hotel. I had an idea.

The TV channel that I had done some property work for also ran a medium type ghost show. I asked the television company to get their medium to come to look at the house. I was always pretty sceptical about such people.

"You know you have a shared house here?"

"We gathered that." I replied. He went around the property feeling, listening and nodding at all sorts of things. He even went out in the garden.

"Tell me something I don't know." I thought to myself.

Later, when he had finished his "survey", I poured him a glass of wine. He asked me lots of questions about the building materials. He was interested in the Indian flagstones, the Welsh slate and the Scottish sandstone in particular.

"You've bought a load of 'em with you, you know."

"A load of what?" I asked.

"Spirits. There are some German ones probably from those beams up there. How old is this stone? Do you know there is a whole farmer's family living here? The Spaniards are not playing good neighbours. They are winding all of 'em up."

"Winding 'em up? Ghosts in building materials?" This was all getting rather silly.

"Well it is rather multi-national, and they don't get on with each other. There is your problem. Spirits can become contained within old materials from the buildings where they used to live. You have imported ghosts from the old properties where these materials came. Normally, you might have heard the odd footstep or moaning over the years but this lot absolutely hate each other. Then when the old Indian guys moved in with the slabs it all kicked off"

I was astounded.

"So what do I do about it exactly?"

"Well we need to scare 'em. We need someone to police the place to keep things quiet. I normally would import an old monk or two. I know just the things…"

I had nothing further to say. Did wine really do this to some people?

He ended up sending me to buy some antique pews from an auction house. They were meant to be very old from some ancient monastery. They did look good, I admit and I placed them in the hall. I wouldn't have been surprised, however, if the auctioneer was a mate of his.

Well I have to hand it to him. It did the trick. By the second night after I placed the pews, there was hardly any sound. We heard the odd groan here and there after that but that was perfectly acceptable in our "old" house.

Soon after, on holiday we both saw the beauty of two ancient swords and shields. They would have looked superb above our fireplace. Previously we would have been tempted, but this time we simultaneously shook our heads and bought a new TV instead.

"Three Strikes and you're out"

A clipboard?

For a prestigious matrimonial agency that supposedly lives by their use of the latest "cutting edge" scientific methods to find permanent matches, Jenny was surprised to see one of the "Senior Consultants" of the exclusive "Love for Keeps" agency sitting untidily in front of her with a clipboard. A pencil was positioned behind his ear. He may as well have been quoting her a price for a fitted carpet.

Still looking only at the papers in front of him, he began.

"I know we asked you this in the questionnaire but we want to be certain, you see. So, thinking back now, and being fully honest now; how many *real* relationships have you had in adult life would you say, er…miss James?"

Jenny had the feeling this question had been repeated by him many times that day.

Dr. Bennett only fully looked up at her after he had referred back to her name again on the top of the sheet.

Those types of questions were never easy to answer to a close friend, let alone to a complete stranger. Without waiting for her to answer, he went on.

"….and in how many of them were you fully in love, would you say …when there was no doubt about it…er…that you, not your partner, were in love. Take your time." He had a funny way of trying to soften the end of each question to make him more approachable yet he always said the word "love" almost as if he needed to cynically prefix it with the word "real".

"Well…" Jenny thought for moment. She stared at a top corner of the room for quite some time. Why do people in thought always look to corners of rooms? Then she looked down at her hands, visibly counting on her fingers.

"About five." She was not sure if it was the exact same answer she gave on the questionnaire.

A furrowed brow and a visible glance at the clock behind her indicated to Jenny that he had lost interest. He had probably observed the finger mathematics.

"And, Miss James....how many times, would you say, have you had your heart broken?"

Trying to appear unsurprised, Jenny tried to answer as best she could remember. Again, he did not look up. The consultant continued to write on his papers. She got the feeling that her answers had not made much difference to the interview outcome and he had already made up his mind after reading her application form.

He was blunt. He was a little cold. She was uncertain as to what discipline Dr. Bennett's doctorate was actually in but he had obvious gaps in his communication skills.

The doctor did not beat about the bush.

"Well, we could find you *a* partner. He may love you, but you will never love him back fully or permanently. It's like this.., and this does come after extensive research by our university team. I'll lend you a copy. You see. The human soul is only capable of actually falling in love a maximum three times over a lifetime. This has now been scientifically proved. Now, Miss James, you've claimed that you have been in love five times in your life. I think that maybe you were obsessed or infatuated for a couple of those love affairs. I think you have almost certainly already used your three opportunities. You might think in the future that you are in love again but you won't really be so and your love for him is not going to last. We want to match our clients mutually so that when they do fall in love hopefully with one another then it will go the distance. We believe that our selected clients fully deserve one another. That's fair, do you see?"

He didn't wait for her answer. Jenny had heard a little about the background of their selection procedure and all this did not come as any surprise.

"I'm afraid it probably wouldn't work for you. You have probably used up your chances now. Three strikes and you are out. That's the way we are doing it, I'm afraid. I'm sorry to be blunt. Now I could take the money and tell you something different, couldn't I?"

Jenny was told that their "sister company, a selective introduction agency" would be able to help her, as she was such a "high quality" applicant. She was told they would write to her and she went home. Disappointed she wasn't, as she hadn't expected much. At her age she had been through a lot.

There were many introduction agencies to choose from. The sector had become big business. It seemed that everyone was single. It seemed that everyone was "dating". Every publication carried adverts for dating agencies and bespoke marriage consultants. A whole industry had emerged which exploited the market of single professional people who were too busy and stressed to devote time and energy to finding a life partner in the traditional way. In recent years it appeared that every relationship became temporary, disposable, and of fixed-term. Long-lasting marriages had become rare. They were so few and far between that they became paradoxically, the new fashionable accessory to aspire to. The "Love for keeps agency" claimed to be different. It did not make guarantees but advertised itself to the world on a manifesto of mutual introductions based exclusively on love itself for selected people. Those carefully selected people taken onto their client list were only those people who would genuinely and naturally fall in love in the future. They maintained that they would admit no one onto their books of who they thought was unlikely to fall in love. Every client was vetted personally and the emphasis of the questioning was on the client's romantic past. There were many applications. Surprisingly, it was not an expensive service. Grants for the service were available from a wealthy benefactor. People had left legacies to the agency on the belief that family values such as marriage would make the world a better place. It had to register as a charity. Jenny had applied for one of the grants. Rather than where other agencies concentrated their efforts on mutually matching people who have as much as possible in common with each another, the "love for keeps" agency based its efforts on the recently proved scientific research into the nature of love itself. It was discovered that the human soul, unless under exceptional circumstances, and discounting childhood "crushes" is only capable of falling in love for at most three times in total.

Jenny had almost forgotten about sending in her application, so long did it take for the agency to respond to her. At the age of 34, she was worried that she would never get the chance to settle down with a stable husband and children. Not that this bothered most people much nowadays. The ever-optimistic Jenny considered herself sentimental and old-fashioned, and had harboured a dream to live like her grandparents had lived; married to each other until death did they part.

That night Jenny lay on her sofa, reading the Sunday newspapers. Her dog stretched reassuringly in front of the fire. It was another one of those anti-climactic Sunday evenings after another disappointing blind date set up by her friends. Unsurprisingly, the man was totally unsuitable. Not so much bothered by the fact that she now knew that it had been scientifically proved that she would probably never feel true love once again but more so by feeling ultimately incomplete; Jenny sighed as another weekend of her life had passed her by. As she went to bed she thought of how fortunate her grandparents had been.

Unread by Jenny in her newspaper was an article arguing that regulatory bodies were needed to audit ethics and standards within some of the service industries' growing sectors. The "Love for keeps" agency had a mention. Jenny missed reading that a Dr Bennett, a senior consultant with the company (and twice divorced) had married one of his handpicked clients at the marriage agency.

Steve Morris

"The best days of our lives"

On paper at least, this particular set of murders looked simple to solve. There had been four of them in less than a year. That they were all linked together there was no doubt. Yet there was no motive whatsoever.

Detective Chief Inspector Brett thought that progress on this investigation was long overdue. They were not particularly grizzly murders. In fact, the strangulations were actually quite surgical. Expertly done. No mess. The same person had killed three men and a woman all aged within one year of each other in exactly the same way. The victims were from very different walks of life and the murders were committed separately in four very different parts of the country. One was in Belgium. The motive was still unknown, DCI Brett's team were no further on and no one knew when or where the next murder would take place. The only link DCI Brett could find between them was that all the victims had possibly lived at one time in a similar area of Leicestershire.

This was a significant link that had been missed previously. The reason being that one of the victims was from a travelling family. Brett checked the dates and facts again, working late into the night.

The third victim must have been barely nine years old when she lived there and then only for less than a year, but she had definitely been around. So, there Brett had a link.

He thought again. He thought about his own life when he was nine years old. He did this often, and they were not all happy memories. He did not particularly enjoy his own schooldays very much.

It seemed obvious to begin the search at a time when all the four victims were first connected together. This was when they were children.

It was a rural area. There weren't many schools in those villages, especially back in the 60s. In fact, at the time there were only two primary schools within twenty miles. He began his search there and checked the records. Fairly quickly, one of Brett's team found out that all four victims had in fact attended the same primary school. This was as Brett had hoped. However, more detailed enquiries were not proving easy.

DCI Brett always considered it amazing just how much of our life story such as work, school and college records get destroyed once it is obsolete. It was an all-too-often scenario in his job. A lot of our life experience is seemingly as disposable and forgettable after its use as our food packaging.

There was a possibility that all four of these murder victims might have even been members of the same school class but facts surrounding the girl were very vague. Travelling pupils were usually quickly forgotten.

Brett was intrigued, puzzled and frustrated. It had to be something other than those early childhood friendships that linked the victims. They must have been connected to each other in later life. Surely the whole primary school class were not going to get assassinated one-by-one?

Reluctantly he visited the school. Brett hated schools at the best of times. He had a distinctly rough time for a few years. Being a late developer and a particularly small child, he stood out from his peers and was bullied continually. He got near to breaking point.

Later as he began to grow properly and as he caught up with his classmates, the bullying faded away but the psychological scars were to remain with him always. The depression and anxiety problems that he had endured in later life had been attributed to his traumatic school days. He always blamed his drinking and subsequent family break up to his traumatic early years.

Brett still shivered when he thought back to those days and was relieved when his search moved on from the school into a records archive at the local education authority.

He examined the class lists in more detail. As a precaution, he took the decision to get his team involved in contacting the former pupils one-by-one without trying to alarm them. One reason for this was simply to check that there had been no further murders of which the police were unaware.

A lot of the former class had, begun by that time, to pick up from the press that four of their former schoolmates had been murdered. The former pupils were all asked if they knew of any further connection between the four victims. Memories were again vague but eventually it was acknowledged by at least two people that the four victims were in fact at some point part of some little "gang" of around five kids. The name of the gang was long forgotten. They did the usual "gang" things that children did, often cruel and often deliberately to the exclusion of other pupils. This was worth considering. Someone could have been taking out the members of this gang one-by-one. If this was significant then fortunately there was only one more member of the gang left to account for. At that point, location of the gang's apparent ringleader was made a priority. It was possible that the murderer had deliberately left this one until last.

The victims of the gang were also researched and where possible, interviewed.

According to some anecdotes, one of the favourite activities of the gang was to continually pick on one small boy called Donald Davidson in the school year below.

Donald Davidson was a particularly sensitive and anxious pupil who was a "born victim" in many ways. Now Brett was getting somewhere. He needed to find more about the gang and more about Davidson. DCI Brett's colleagues did not agree with his line of inquiry and were looking more towards a possible teenage link between the victims. How could anyone bear a grudge for so long, especially over such childish incidents?

The one remaining member of the gang, Smith, was entirely unaware of the murders of his former friends. When Brett questioned him, Smith, now a nightclub owner, could hardly even remember the names of the other members of his one-time gang. He could, however, still remember cruelties dished out to little Davidson. He still couldn't help a chuckle. The DCI did not share his amusement.

Davidson's location was soon traced but he was not around to be questioned.

By all accounts Davidson was apparently an introvert and a lifelong loner. He worked in IT. He was paranoid and was obsessed with security, self-defence and martial arts. Like Brett thought at the start, this case was simple. A classic profile.

Round the clock surveillance was placed upon Smith on a shift system.

The break-in happened on the watch of DCI Brett. Davidson was seen to enter Smith's premises through an open window. This was it. Brett followed. Maybe Davidson knew that he was being watched himself. Maybe Davidson didn't care.

Brett followed very slowly.

He did nothing. He looked at Davidson. He said nothing.

Davidson continued.

Brett and Davidson looked at one another.

Nothing needed to be said.

Brett watched the life fade out of the ringleader Smith under Davidson's grip.

"He is the last one, isn't he?" Asked Brett

The executioner nodded.

Brett thought back to his schooldays again. He had been driven close to suicide several times. This was to stay with him for his life. He understood.

Looking away from Davidson, Brett stepped aside.

"I got here five minutes too late." He said as Davidson brushed past him.

"Go. Now. But there are to be no more." Said Brett

The executioner nodded then left quickly.

Brett was not going to be responsible to catch this guy this time.

"Revenge on a plate"

They were spitting hate. Their gums peeled back to reveal the roots of their teeth. In the cold floodlit garden, even their visible breath threatened to kill. Their glazed eyes tunnelled directly ahead. They were becoming difficult to hold.

Six powerful front legs shook with fury. Their jet-black nails were scraping madly at the gravel.

They had now ceased barking and all three were growling deeply. Their low growls came not from their mouths but instead from somewhere deep inside them. I knew I couldn't hold them for much longer.

The two Dobermans had heard the intruders first. Only half awake at 3:00AM, I slipped them onto their leashes and turned on the security lights. I could now hear the dogs' sets of teeth stapling together rapidly. I often wondered how their tongues survived unscathed in the middle of that razor battlefield. The Pit Bull, always a good ten seconds behind the other two was now puffed up with a chest as wide as his length. Even in the night, the line of white skin beneath his black fur was visible all along his back as his spinal hair was raised vertically. He made vile gagging noises as his throat strained against his chain. He spun around and yanked wildly in a frantic attempt to free himself of his constraint. As he wrapped the leash around my legs I felt he was as rigid as a barrel of oil and twice as heavy. I realised his body had tensed so solidly that there was not a square centimetre of loose flesh anywhere upon him. I really was not able to hold these three any longer. The dogs were now literally dragging me to their prey.

The two Dobermans with their nostrils visibly pulsating were snapping violently at the burglars as if to suck them closer. Now they were cornered, the dogs could now taste the very fear in their prey.

I saw it in my mind. The Dobermans' first strike would be in seconds. Trapped in our grounds, they could not outrun these pair. I knew they would leap up at the intruders to do their initial damage. I knew they would firstly snap at anything hanging like vulnerable fingers, or even their stomachs with their wicked white little razors. These were intelligent animals. They had made their minds up earlier exactly where they were going to hit first. But in theory strong men could still fight them off. They had not got the power to produce anything instantly permanent against a strong intruder. That was why I bought in the other one for our protection. I had to make sure. He took a long time to find. He was a huge male Pit Bull crossed with something even larger. After they saw me training him, my friends pleaded with me to get rid of "that thing" before someone got seriously hurt. I kept him chained up most of the time and didn't let the kids play with him.

He was a massive specimen. When he took hold of his prey, there was no chance of him ever letting go. It was simply "to the end" with that one. He was exceptionally powerful. His muscles shone through his gloss black steel coat. He crunched most dog bones like they were mints. In fact as soon as he got his adult teeth I had to even stop giving him ox-knuckle bones as he ran the risk of choking on the splinters he made. He was an insurance policy in the event that the intruders were armed. You see; he didn't feel any pain. You could probably sever one of his legs cleanly off and I knew that he would still not let go.

I knew that if he was fortunate enough to take one of their lower legs in a single grip then that was that. It would be over. Their fibulas would break quite quickly. If not on the first bite then the second securing snap would break them no problem. Such were the size of his jaws that I fancied that, if he took his best grip, both the leg bones would go at once. I could see it in my mind. Then they would be down and then they would be ours.

The police had told me that statistically at least, these particular intruders would probably be back to take more of our things. They gave me some security advice but it was mostly about prevention and alarm equipment. I wanted revenge.

I had worked hard. I was now famous. We were a wealthy family. We had many nice things. But our things were ours. They should not have done what they did when they broke in last year. They should not have done what they did to our little Westie when they burgled our house. What if one of the kids had been home alone when they came in? Now it was their fault and they were about to pay.

They were now in front of me pleading.

They were quite literally begging. They now knew they had made a big mistake coming back. The Dobermans' saliva sparkled against the security beam. One of them lunged and lunged at the scumbags, each time gagging against its collar. They knew that with their next lunge they would penetrate the nearest intruder's throat. All would be worth it. For me. For the family. For the dogs. For our home. For our possessions. For our old dog. I screamed obscenities. They had to know just what damned evil garbage they were before they met their end.

"Please don't let 'em go mister."

My wife screamed "No. For God's sake, No!" from the upstairs window.

I didn't reply. I was literally seconds away from seeing a lot of blood.

I had waited a long time for it. It was what I had prepared for. They were the ones. I could recognise them from the police descriptions.

I just wanted them torn to red ribbons. My two central right fingers holding the Dobermans' chain were nearly broken. The Terrier leash I had wrapped around my middle. It was getting difficult to breathe.

One of the Dobermans was almost there. He reached out at them with his beautiful front incisors. One of the burglars was by then visibly urinating.

I had convinced myself I would do it ever since that time we got burgled.

I was still in control. I did not have to go through with it even then.

I had thought about this probably every single night in the last year. I had convinced myself to go through with it if I ever caught them. But I had given little thought to what would happen afterwards.

My lovely dogs would be destroyed. I would be prosecuted. I might be imprisoned. My career and celebrity status would be over. If I was to let those things loose then I would pay for this for many years to come. It would probably be manslaughter. These two were very very scared. Maybe that was enough. Maybe they had learned their lesson already. Our kids needed their dad. Maybe even these two pieces of low life had kids.

All of a sudden a door crashed open violently behind me, and there was a commotion. I frantically turned to see three police officers running through our conservatory and sliding onto the gravel behind me.

Momentarily startled, and off balance it was too late for me and I lost my grip…

"Better late than never"

"Well I never quite got around to it" was Benson's usual reply.

This was the answer Benson generally gave when he was asked the reason why he had never got married or had a family. He actually did get a little tired of being asked that particular question. He wished people wouldn't ask it.

"I've always been too busy" and "I never met anyone quite nice enough" were other excuses he gave. Why did people have to assume that there was something wrong with being a lifelong bachelor?

You see Benson had been a fully qualified "bachelor" for all his life. Admittedly, he *had* always kept a busy life. No one could really argue with that. In addition to his work as a graphic designer, he kept himself busy, perhaps deliberately, with amateur dramatics, painting and sculpture among many other things. Benson was almost sixty-six. He was a man who was always on the move. He was friendly to everybody but never had a lot of time for people, seemingly to be perpetually late. It was as if his watch had been set thirty minutes behind time years ago and he had never got round to putting it right. To his neighbours, Benson was a pleasant, well-spoken, slightly eccentric type who generally "kept himself to himself". This was probably because he found it difficult to mix with people who weren't "his kind" of people. "His kind" of people were those who had a genuine passion for art and who could see the same qualities in art that he could see. According to those around him, he could do with "tidying up his appearance, his garden and his house a bit" but above all he was regarded as a man you could trust. Often this is the way of a bachelor.

In his work, Benson had done quite well for himself. He took early retirement, kept up with his artistic interests and was as busy as ever he was at work. He regularly took vacations as a member of artists' workshops and retreats often in France and Spain.

Was he truly happy? Well, Benson never complained, not even about single supplements.

One day something very different happened. Mary had joined a residential sculpture class at the same time as him. Shoulders did literally bump as both artists found themselves admiring the sunset from a balcony. No other members of the class had noticed it during the interval or else thought it worth looking at. Both stood transfixed for minutes unaware of each other's company, until Mary first broke the silence as they admired the amazing beauty of the end of that day. "Yes. Just what I was thinking." Were Benson's first words to Mary.

Mary was very interesting. She was similarly single, similarly unique and with obvious similar interests. The next lunchtime they chatted over coffee. Talking about his art, Benson was always pleasantly enthusiastic and easy to talk to. He could see that Mary was genuinely interested in the subject and not just studying art to pass the time in her retirement years. She could see things that Benson could see. The conversation with Mary flowed easily. Mary was pleasant to talk to. She also disliked people who were not on her Bohemian artistic level so for her, talking to Benson was a rare connection.

He enjoyed that first lunchtime company with Mary. However, at Benson's stage in life, he had met literally hundreds of new people over hundreds of lunches, connected well, felt good and then nothing ever came further of it. He was used to that. A man of his experience was unlikely to become over-excited by anything new really. At his stage of life he had seen it all before.

With Mary, however, things developed. He realised that he had never met anyone quite like Mary before and never expected that he would do. With so very much in common, they were to connect especially closely. They soon began to see each other regularly. Then, despite his best preventative attempts, Benson developed *feelings* for Mary.

"Feelings? Me? How on earth am I going to fit Mary into my routine?" He thought.

Well, it was funny exactly just how he did manage to move things around to accommodate Mary. People in love do that. When he had a million and one things to do, the "million and second" job of seeing Mary was rapidly promoted to the top of his "to do" list. He amazed himself. He was sixty-six and he was behaving like he was sixteen again. That was the last time when he had shown any interest in women.

After six months of seeing Mary, he wondered exactly how he had managed without her all that time. She had a good effect on Benson. He soon became tidier, took far more care with his appearance and even began to cut his lawns regularly. His neighbours liked Mary.

Benson was now changed. He reconsidered his lifelong cynicism towards women. Instead of trying to fool himself he was happy; he decided that he had at last found a happiness that was tangible and genuine.

With Mary, as well as the great affection they felt for each other, they had very many things in common. Being of similar age, they grew up witnessing the very same things as each other. One Sunday, they reminisced about holidays in the fifties at a time when they were both teenagers.

"This is a photo of my very first holiday without my parents." She said, pointing to an almost sepia-coloured browned photo. "I was a teenager and I went away with these five girls from the school. We had a great time in Brighton." Benson imagined that Mary would have been an incredibly pretty girl at that time. She would have attracted a lot of attention in those days.

Brighton was a popular holiday destination in the fifties. They compared notes about the fashion and music of those times. Looking back, Mary and Benson were amazed just how people actually could think they looked good with those haircuts.

Mary remembered one summer in fifty-six that had been particularly hot. Maybe her nostalgic memory had added a few degrees to the temperature. The country was optimistically back on its feet after the problems of the previous decade. People were in a good mood and during that summer the south coast weather was obligingly good for the whole summer long. She recalled one day when after seemingly spending the whole day involved seriously in ice cream, fish-and-chips and laughter, they made their way to the funfair. With a lump in her throat, the nostalgic Mary was still even able to smell and taste the very salt and vinegar of that afternoon. They had been followed around by a bunch of lads all that morning. By Mary's own admission, they did not try particularly hard to get away from their pursuers. Shared candyfloss and mixed doubles on the dodgem cars soon followed.

"Yes, Dodgems were great. You could actually bump people in those days" reminisced Benson.

"We had such a nice time that we arranged to meet the lads next day. They all seemed really well mannered and reliable. Boys like that seemed always difficult to meet. We were really disappointed when they stood us up outside the pictures next afternoon. We only had two days left."

"Still. Never mind. I've got my memories." Said the elegant Mary looking somewhere into the distance. "No one can take those away from me. Oh, and a couple of photos of the week"

Benson tilted the first faded photograph to the light.

He saw that sat next to Mary on the dodgem car in Brighton was a clean cut young Benson.

Steve Morris

"The Brand New Colour"

"Just how I am supposed to describe a colour to you that is totally new?" Old Riley asked frustrated. "Just how do I do it....?" He didn't expect an answer and he never got one.

He was sitting in his familiar wheelchair in the lounge of The Acorn Retirement home in Coventry. The old man frequently became agitated at this point of his story.

He never quite grew tired of talking to new people at length about how he had once discovered a magical "new colour". Old Riley was often frustrated, however, when asked to describe the colour itself. This was more so now as since he had lost the remainder of his sight. His memory remained fully intact.

I was at the retirement home often around that time as my wife worked there for a while. Old Riley's story begins nearly seventy years ago.

In the years during the war, Riley was bought up in a small village just outside the city of Coventry. He was a shy and lonely boy but lived for the summer holidays, which he often spent fishing, rambling, shooting and generally pottering around in those particularly hot summers, which we all seemed to have had in our childhoods. One day I'll check those actual weather records.

Some details of the story he was more clear about than others.

One hot afternoon while rambling through the countryside looking for either mischief or amusement, he found himself alongside a field where there was a group of young people playing rounders and laughing loudly. From what he could remember, the group was approximately half boys and half girls a little older than him, and there was nothing extraordinary in that. Kids played more healthy outdoor games in those days. The group seemed foreign to him somehow and were generally fair-haired and tall. They were all of particularly healthy appearance, very attractive and all seemed to be having a good time. This seemed significant to him, then being the early years of the Second World War.

Riley stood by the field watching them for a little while. One particular solid hit by one of the boys saw the ball rolling near to where Riley was standing. He bent down to pick it up. He was instantly struck by what a strange colour the ball was. Before he had more time to look at it, and being a very nervous lad he thought he had better get it back to the team that very instant. He was amazed that he had found the courage to even pick it up.

A teenage girl came running up to Riley and he gently threw it back to her hand.

"Thanks" she smiled as she wiped the sweat from her brow.

"We're one short on our team if you fancy a game." She suggested.

Riley nodded, as shy as he was. He was pleased with himself for having the confidence to accept. The group seemed nice. Rounders was easy.

"Good. You can field here. We'll be in bat soon".

"I've got a new player for our side." She shouted as she threw the curious ball to the bowler.

The game restarted. It went on for all afternoon. They stopped for regular breaks when they had drinks and sweet fruit. Usually time flies by while we are enjoying ourselves but that afternoon seemed to go on forever.

They were all interested in Riley and asked him a lot of questions as he enjoyed their fruit. He was asked so many questions about his life that he did not get much chance to ask much of them, concentrating on catching all their names and hearing their jokes. He was a shy boy anyway.

One question, he did manage to get in.

"Where are you all from then?"

"Oh we're not from around here. We're just visiting for a little while." One of the lads answered without even looking at Riley. It was time to restart the play.

The sun carried on shining; the game of rounders turned into other different new sports and the day went on.

It was, quite simply, the best day of Riley's short life.

Eventually, becoming aware of the time and the distance to walk back, Riley decided he had better set off for home before his parents began to worry about him.

He bade farewell to his new friends, said he hoped to see them again and began reluctantly walking away.

Just then he noticed that he was still carrying one of their uniquely coloured balls in his hand. Riley shouted back that they should catch it as he threw it.

"Keep it! Souvenir!" The girl who had initially spoke to him casually shouted back.

So he went on his way home.

As he examined the ball that night, he was unable to sleep. The very different colour, to this day, he still cannot describe. The simple reason for this was that the colour did not exist. It was not like red, nor blue nor yellow. It was neither part of our rainbow nor of any spectrum. Ryan had never seen any flower, any fish or anything of any similar colour. How could that happen? It was not in the rainbow. It was not a mixture of any of our colours.

He decided to find out more about the ball and the children. Sadly, that was not easy due to the escalation of the war and air raids, which were becoming a common occurrence in Coventry. They had begun in earnest in recent weeks and his parents did not like the idea that he should venture too far alone.

As soon as he did get the opportunity, he decided to try to locate his newly found friends. He found the field where they had played easily enough but there was no sign of the youngsters to be found anywhere. He asked some locals if they had seen them but no one had seemed to recognise his descriptions of them.

So, had it all been a dream? He did dream a lot, often in the day, as was written on his school report each and every year. But then he had the ball. It was his prize possession. No one else had a ball like that. No one else, except for his new friends. He was convinced.

Riley fingered it carefully in his pocket. He had to keep it safe. He would never let it out of his sight. It would be kept under his pillow while he slept.

The events of the next few days were vague for Riley. He would be thankful for this blurring of his memory in future years. Perhaps it was for the best. Mother Nature could be kind as well as cruel.

During a particularly heavy assault by German bombers, the street where the Riley family lived took a couple of heavy impacts. The whole street became an inferno. The warning came too late and residents did not get to the shelters in time.

Riley must have been knocked unconscious. A fireman carried him from his bed. By all accounts it was a miraculous escape. Young Riley was one of the lucky few to escape with their lives from the street that night.

When he regained consciousness, he found that the rest of his family had been killed in the raid that night.

Riley was, like many others from then on, changed in many ways.

The unrecognisable street was a pile of reeking wet black soot. It smouldered for days and days. Of course he looked for the ball. His house was barely remaining let alone individual items. Anything and everything was lost.

That was seventy years ago. His eyes, even in his blindness, still filled up when he got to that point of the story. He had told his tale countless times to anyone who would listen. It always affected him in the same way.

Last week, we all heard of the discovery. During an archaeological dig in Syria, what are turning out to be the oldest-ever supposed man-made artefacts have been unearthed. They predate pretty much everything that had ever been found in the region or anywhere on Earth. Still shrouded in mystery, early indications are that the relics are from some previously undiscovered civilisation. The world has to change the way it looks at its own past. The history books are being re-written.

There is emerging evidence of some balls, some wonderful balls. These balls are apparently a miraculous new colour. Science books were now being re-thought. Thousands are flocking to catch a glimpse of them. The world's press are in a frenzy.

Last night, I wanted to be the first to tell Old Riley. He always had time for me and would listen. I couldn't wait and I phoned in the middle of the night. He wouldn't mind.

"Oh, Mr. Riley sadly passed away three months ago." Came the reply from the nurse.

Still, Old Riley had been right all along.

"Dreamer"

Martin Peters the promising young architect woke at his normal time of 7:40 AM. The alarm clock did not buzz but he never needed it to anyway. It was always the same. He had set his body clock to wake himself at that time every day without fail. Such was his routine.

He liked getting up in the morning. Martin was a positive person. He felt sure that the day would be a good day. Promotion was imminent and he wanted to get to work as soon as possible in hope of receiving the official notification of his long-held ambition.

Something was wrong.

He looked around his bedroom and didn't recognize a thing. Things didn't feel like they were his. At that point, Martin Peters remembered that he was, in fact, Malcolm Harris and that he had all that night been dreaming he was a man called Martin Peters.

That he had been dreaming was obvious. What was not so clear was just how long he had been dreaming. He knew every intimate detail of Martin Peters' life inside out; from his childhood memories, through schools; to his career in architecture. He had memories of seemingly every event of Peters' life. He knew what time he took the morning train and what brand of deodorant he used. Bizarrely, he even knew the previous brand of deodorant Peters had used. He must have been dreaming for a long time. That could be the only explanation.

How could he remember so much?

The telephone rang and he answered it.

"Good morning sleepy head."

"Ah...Diane," He replied recognising his girlfriend.

"Just ringing to check you are alright. You were really tired on your way home last night. You couldn't keep your eyes open."

"Yes. I'm fine."

He had obviously had an early night and had slept heavily.

"Good. Just checking you are awake. You know how you are sometimes. See you at work. Bye!"

Malcolm replaced the receiver remembering that Martin Peters was a bachelor although he was once engaged to an American girl. How on earth did he know this? Who was Peters exactly?

It was only a dream. A big dream.

A detail he did remember was that Martin Peters didn't dream very often but had once suffered vivid nightmares on recovering from a nasty operation.

Malcolm Harris was a journalist working for an evening newspaper. He hated his job.

Slowly he got ready for work and began to do battle with the London traffic. He wished then that he were indeed Martin Peters; the headhunted architect who was now turning down job offers all the time. Martin Peters enjoyed his job.

At work, Harris told his colleagues all about his dream.

"If your dream was so comprehensive, then perhaps you even know where this Martin Peters lives," Suggested Diane

"29, Fir Tree Avenue, Slough," he replied, as quickly as he could have repeated his own address.

"I suppose you know his phone number?" she went on.

"818160," Harris replied indifferently.

"Then give him a ring and see if he really exists," Suggested the ingenious Diane

"And what would I say exactly? 'Hello. I am Malcolm Harris. I've just been dreaming I was you. I know what you had for supper last night'? He'd think I was crazy!"

What Harris did, however, was to telephone directory enquiries to confirm the existence of the enigmatic Mr. Peters. Malcolm did not want to talk to him. That would have been a very bizarre conversation.

"No such an address or number for a Mr. Peters. No such an address in Slough, actually." Returned the operator.

So that was that. It had all been a dream and he did not exist at all and probably never had. Malcolm Harris decided that he was still and always had been Malcolm Harris then went about his usual day in his usual way.

At about 5 O'clock he began to miss the life of Peters. He knew everything that Peters had planned for that evening and in some way felt envious and even homesick. He simply wished he was Peters.

As he settled down for the evening, an interesting thought suddenly occurred to him. Perhaps he was Martin Peters all along and now he was only dreaming of being Malcolm Harris. However, like before, he could remember every detail of his life history, as Malcolm Harris so therefore could not be dreaming that. In fact, by the end of the evening he wasn't sure exactly which of the two men he was. Which man had dreamed the dream of which other?

He went to sleep in a very troubled, confused and concerned manner. It was any wonder he got to sleep at all.

He awoke next morning fully aware that he had been dreaming again.

"Gary, are you getting up or what? " Came the voice of his wife standing by the door.

"Enchantment"

He was always very different. Some people just are.

From the very first day of class, he was certainly an outsider. The other lads in particular disliked him. The girls didn't find him cool. Such is the way of the schoolyard that "Weirdo" and "Warlock" were often words used to Lucien's face in an attempt to provoke him. Yet, he never responded.

I found him fascinating. Yet I couldn't tell him that. I was far too shy and I never told the other girls of my fascination. So I was destined to admire him from afar and to wonder whom, if anyone, he was actually close to.

Lucien was, from what little we knew, an orphan. He lived with his elderly grandfather who owned a little land, in a ramshackle old farmhouse out near the woods. The farm had long since stopped operating and only the signs of smoke rising from the chimney and slight light through windows indicated that anyone actually lived there. He was a loner at school and would often spend long periods absent. We had no idea how he got away with that. Lucien kept himself to himself.

The farmhouse itself would be called "private" by most estate agents. It was not somewhere where anyone routinely passes by on the way to anywhere. The driveway was overgrown and the wooden gates rotten. This was why we never really saw much of Lucien outside of school.

He was never seen around town. Occasionally we would catch glimpses of him in the fields by the edge of the woods. He was obviously into hunting and falconry as usually when we saw him, he had some large bird of prey tethered to his arm. Scratches on his knuckles were signs of close contact with his birds.

I saw him once while walking my dogs near there. He looked particularly impressive on one of those autumn dusks when the wind is still mild. His long hair and the falcon's tail feathers were blowing as two synchronised outlines against the departing sun. That night the wind was reading its own agenda of the oncoming winter.

I admit that I often used dog walks as an excuse to walk near to the old cottage. I wanted to find out more about Lucien and his life. He was so different. The other kids at school were too predictable in their obsessions with the latest jeans, computer games and cider. I didn't like conformists.

My parents always encouraged me to be healthy and to get as much outdoor exercise as I could. This was one of the reasons they bought me two lovely Irish setters, Sheba and Dasher. Too busy to walk them, my parents gave me full responsibility for the dogs. This was meant to be good for me. As it happened, it worked out well and I enjoyed being in charge of them. By return Sheba and Dasher were loyal, healthy and looked after me.

One Saturday morning while returning from a good run with them, I spied someone who I thought was Lucien in the clearing at the edge of the woods. It was some way off but I was convinced that what looked like two large black birds swooped down out of the trees to him to eat out of his hand. They must have been two of his birds of prey. Then the moment was gone and I could see him no more.

A few weeks later came to be my first encounter with the enigmatic Lucien outside school. Ironically, it came at a time when as teenage life got more pressured and busy, I was beginning to forget about him.

Dasher was off colour; so I took Sheba, my female dog, out on her own.

As I approached a corner at the edge of the wood, Sheba dropped to the ground and put her head between her front paws. I could not move her. She was a bouncy character and this was very unlike her.

I came face to face with Lucien coming the other way around the corner. The tall youth was dressed in khaki colours, boots and a scarf. He kept his head down and avoided eye contact with me. He did look at Sheba as he walked past. I had to speak.

"Hiya." I said.

He nodded, carried on walking and kept looking at Sheba.

"Nice morning..." I was struggling to start a conversation. "Been far?"

"Where's the other? She looks worried about the other one. He's not well." He replied still looking only at Sheba.

"What? How do you know...?"

"She...I just guessed."

Two owls hooted nearby somewhere. Sheba was still lying in a submissive position but did not seem afraid. Her tail wagged. She tilted her head continually from side-to-side as if concentrating carefully on every word. Lucien seemed to look at Sheba in preference to me.

"Best to get the male checked out quick"
"Yes, we will." I replied. Then I tried again to start a conversation.
"Thought about your 5th year options yet?"
He shrugged his shoulders and shook his head.
"I'd better get going. Don't forget what I said"
"Bye"
He walked off. That was that.

Dasher, was no better that night and we ended up rushing him to the vet. He was found to have an intestinal obstruction. He had eaten something plastic that must have become stuck on its way through. The vet said that he had seen many dogs die from that problem. I was close to my dogs and remember that I got quite upset until the next morning when I heard that the operation had been successful.

I did not see Lucien again for a while, as it was then the beginning of the summer holidays.

As a family we went abroad for four weeks. I thought about him often. Teenagers are like that, as you know.

The local paper had some interesting news on our return. A new bypass was proposed right through the woodland. It was planned to pass through land owned by Lucien's grandfather, the land was to be compulsorily purchased and he was refusing to move. I admired his defiant attitude but local residents thought the bypass a good idea. It would remove a lot of traffic from the town.

There now follows the most remarkable series of events in my life that has lived with me up to this day. I have never before spoken about it and before you ask, no I don't know where he ended up. It began on a Sunday on yet another dog walk.

I saw him through the trees. Yes, there he was. I tried to get closer by creeping carefully into the wood. The dogs were sure footed but with my heavy clumsy footsteps I stepped deafeningly, on a twig. A large bird crowed noisily from above me. Lucien must have heard me. Then, he looked in my direction. He carried on. I think he knew I was there. It would seem as if he wanted to be seen.

I saw then fully what was going on. Lucien was feeding animals. This was not like throwing breadcrumbs to pigeons. Twenty wild birds were sat on his arms, back and head. Red squirrels and a rabbit buzzed around his feet. Birds of all types flew back up to branches and more flew down again in some sort of happy civilised queue.

Then, bizarrely, appeared a fox. This was no coincidence. It was an impossibility of wildlife like nothing else I have ever seen. It was as if all the magic of the world was charmed on this very place for a moment in time. Why? Another fox brushed past my legs like a domestic cat as it casually joined the meeting. I was amazed at how smooth it felt. It seemed I was an invited witness to this dream-like enchantment. There were creatures everywhere. Everything was moving. Yet, I couldn't intrude further on him there. I could not disturb all this. That would have clearly been wrong. I quietly led the remarkably docile dogs away and out of the woods.

Sunday was a dream, obviously.

The following week at school was not easy. The atmosphere in our year group had been deteriorating over time. There had been some violent incidents. Expulsions happened weekly and gangs were forming. Instead of enjoying our final year of school there were a lot of feudal revenge attacks brewing and scores left unsettled. The newspaper article gave lads in the class a good excuse to goad Lucien. Pupils taunted him all week long about it. He did his best to turn his back but the harassment just got worse and worse particularly on Friday. It was an uncomfortably humid day. Lucien looked distantly out of the window visibly resenting the time he was wasting in school. Large crows in the schoolyard had somehow replaced the gulls picking at litter after break.

"What's your problem about moving out of that house, tramp?"

"I'm talking to you weirdo." A boy said as he shoved Lucien sharply in the back.

The pushes became more and more violent in the corridors. Lucien was a big lad himself and something obviously was going to give before the end of the day. The sky was becoming dark and heavy, the temperature warm and it was humid. A storm would surely break before the end of the day.

I deliberately brushed past him, put my hand on his arm and told him quietly to "Ignore them, Lucien."

This was proving to be difficult. I went to try to alert a member of staff.

The taunting became worse during last period. The teacher left early to perform their "gate duty", but probably was as keen as us to end school for the day to escape to our outside lives. As we all left the classroom, Lucien found himself trapped at the back.

"Gypsy scum. They're gonna bulldoze your house....and we don't want you here" said an aggressive, hot and bothered lad called Marcus.

"So do us all a favour and get lost now" he continued, this time pushing Lucien violently backward.

Catching him off-balance this time, he fell backward over a desk and a fight broke out. They were both strong lads full of energy. The noise was deafening. Lucien was getting the better of Marcus.

Suddenly, one lad with Marcus pulled out a knife. Lucien realised the change in odds, and dived out through an open window. Black crows scavenging under the classroom window scattered into the air. He ran across the yard, over a fence and headed out of town. Three of the lads gave chase. I followed as best I could.

Lucien, a strong runner, was ahead but his tormentors were gaining. He was heading homewards.

The wind began to swirl as the light fell.

Lucien was slowing as he neared the woods.

As I rounded the corner I saw he had stopped dead and turned to face them. Lucien's face was pale like a moon. His expression had changed. I swear to this day that the sky behind Lucien was jet black.

That sky was full.

That angry black sky was polluted.

In that angry black horizon I could see behind Lucien and behind the boys that chased him, as all figures had stopped dead and odds were again reversed.

I could see behind them only the claws and the beaks of two thousand crows and ravens.

I turned homewards. That was no dream.

Steve Morris

"Quiet life"

Dean's parents owned a passive photography shop and after they died, he took on all the responsibility of that. He often felt unfulfilled living his whole life in the village where he was born but he ran the shop out of loyalty to his family and to his regular customers.

The shop sold cameras, lenses, provided film processing and did some restoration services. It was a slow business in an even slower street. One thing that Dean always said was that "Nothing ever happens" there. He became a dull man who followed routines and he faded and greyed almost into one of his restored sepia photographs.

It was a Sunday evening when the news story broke. It was centred on a large private country estate that adjoined Dean's village. It was to be breaking news that after which, made all future breaking newsflashes seem trivial or just spin-offs from "the story". The breaking of the story was to be a monumental change in modern history. From that day on, time and dates were measured only from either before or after "it happened". Everyone remembered exactly where they were the moment they first heard the news. The initial headlines were then set to dominate each and every news headline for ten years and more. Short of breakouts of war and the Kennedy story it was to be one of our biggest ever bad-news events and then more significantly, one of the world's biggest mysteries. All other subsequent news stories were then not really deemed newsworthy and went on quietly and briefly in the background.

Dean talked of nothing else with his customers all the next day. The general consensus was that the authorities knew who they were after; they would probably at that time be trying to flee the country and would be in custody by teatime.

Living in our media-driven society even entire TV and radio channels were set up to update and debate rolling news developments in the story. It was without media precedent. Someone had assassinated our "Celebrity" teenage twin Princes. Someone had shot both of the young "Hell-Raisers" while they were out riding on the country estate. Who, though?

Apparently it was done clinically at long range by a high-velocity telescopic rifle. Of course the nation immediately went into turmoil and the press into frenzy. Everything and anything stood still for weeks and months. People's daily lives and routines changed permanently from that time on. Nobody seemed to talk of anything else. Yet there were no charges bought. There was seemingly no evidence. As hours moved into days then weeks, the investigation went on and on without result. The trail had gone cold. Evidence was leading absolutely nowhere and no credible groups had claimed responsibility. Searches in the area had led to nothing. Under pressure to make arrests, at one stage, the British and European secret services were hauling in terrorist after terrorist and infiltrating extremist-groups right, left and centre. The few leads they had all pointed towards some isolated radical terrorist cell, consisting of only a few individuals. Massive counter-terrorist offensives were implemented overseas. Every country with recent links to fundamental terrorism was then full of British military. For once, there was no shortage of troops. Every young man was angry. A generation of men looking for revenge was spawned. Enlistment to serve in the military was at record levels. We were then, in essence, at war with many enemies at once.

DNA forensic profiling and "Human Rights" lawyers cleared every single suspect without genuine evidence. The trail had gone dead and conspiracy theories had become rife.

The television companies endlessly debated security failings. Ironically, all procedures were proved to have been followed. It was as if the assassin had disappeared into thin air.

Rather than "Morning...", "All right?" "Nice weather" etc. most people greeted each other with "Any news?". After a while, there never really were any further developments but instead of the story just blurring into obscurity, it made people even more determined for a conclusion. The whole thing went on for so long that children were born, grew up with and even thought about their oncoming teenage years all under the shadow of "The Princes Mystery."

Dean, like most other people, found himself addicted to each and every broadcast. He went to bed at night only after watching the very last news bulletin that his eyelids would allow. Like many others, he felt frustrated at having to sleep at night in case any new development was made in the night. Needless to say, the first thing he did in the morning was to eagerly concentrate on updates of the overnight news. Like the silver lining around the cloud of war times, it did bring people together and did give everyone a focus. Then, at other times, he became bored with a thousand and one angles on the same story, day in - day out.

Dean became one of the many millions of people who became obsessed with debating wild theories around "The Princes Mystery". To make conversation and to help break the routine of his otherwise tedious days, he discussed it with everyone who came into the shop. Everyone had something to say about it and all had their own opinions about who was ultimately behind the crime. New theories and supposed "information leaks from credible sources" often came and went but each media development lasted only a couple of days before it was discounted. There was seemingly never any substance.

The press set up permanent bases in their pretty "chocolate box" village. After the initial novelty of having the outside attention, their large vans and their satellite dishes in the village soon began to spoil the environment of the classic rural views. Dean could now only see only white porta-cabins and satellite dishes rather than his previous view of thatched roofs and a duck pond. It was an ill wind, as they say, however. Some local storekeepers welcomed the increase in trade. New stores began to be built to cope with the increase in demand. Catering vans and their litter were "sore thumbs". Dean actively campaigned with other residents against the planning permissions for these new buildings. It was all becoming rather tedious.

After the first year and when the world's press showed no sign of moving, Dean and other village residents began to regret the days they used to complain that "nothing interesting ever happened there". Usually, even major news stories in those days were so temporary and disposable. However there was no way that this story was ever going to become "yesterday's fish and chips". It just went on and on. One major event had happened in the long history of the village. It was not a happy event. The name of the village would be forever associated with one thing and one thing only.

For Dean, it was time to move on. He had worked in the family business for twenty-five years. This was about twenty years too long. He should have done many other things in his life, than live in that village. A new start was needed.

He fitted in the last few boxes into his hired van.

As he closed the rear door, Dean glanced at the box, which contained the black rifle's case.

"Perfect"

I often wish I had done more about it at the time. I was completely captivated. I had never seen a face like hers. The way she danced totally transfixed me. Then came her voice with her beautiful harmonies. It was a hot night and I felt warm inside. She was just right. To me at least, she was perfect. In a moment everything clicked and I then knew exactly what I had always been looking for. There she was and I knew I would always remember her. But she was only on my TV singing with a foreign band, alas.

That Friday night I arrived home travel-weary and I decided to collapse into bed as soon as I could. Twelve hours later, when I finally came downstairs again, I got on with the new busy day, not really thinking about her again until I had time to recover and gather my thoughts that next afternoon. It was like I had somehow recorded the performance digitally in my mind. And that vivid image would stay clearly in my memory for a decade.

Ten years further down the line, my life had obviously moved on. I had done pretty well for myself and it was, satisfyingly, mostly due to my own efforts. I had found success and it felt good.

I was still single. That made the decision easier, that for no other particular reason than to "get her out of my system" I decided that I had to find her. However clichéd that may sound, I felt that unless I actually went ahead and did this then life would simply not be fulfilled. I had never really done anything spontaneously "reckless" in my life. I resolved to meet her. Then I could move on. Job done.

By then, good fortune had given me the means to find her. What was the worst thing that could happen? What had I got to lose? Well, she might have hated me or told me I was ugly! I am sure I could have accepted that. My search began.

Maybe I should start from the beginning. My name is John Winters. I am 39 years old and I was at that time working as an all-round IT repairman. I fixed hardware, software and all manner of people's seemingly irreparable gadget problems. People liked me for that.

I had been away on a great summer holiday and had returned home that Friday after a long seventeen hours of stop-start delays. I was drowsy, numb, sunburned, and unshaven with my mind busily lagging behind me somewhere in a different time zone. I was, however, in an especially good mood of satisfaction. Without doubt, it was the best holiday I had ever had with close friends and there was still plenty of summer sun left to look forward to here in the UK so I was in exactly the right frame of mind to be receptive to an exceptionally striking face. That night I flicked on the TV while my eyelids would still let in some light, and there she was. Wow.

The time itself was in early summer 1996. It was some obscure late-night music show discovered randomly by flicking through channels. One of the guest bands was a New Zealand group obviously in the UK for a week to promote what was to be a trial song release. My subsequent research found that they did that TV show, had some radio and video play, had a very minor chart hit and then disappeared back to New Zealand never to be seen again. Their fusion of rap and jazz did not fit any of the then UK dance or pop markets. I did not see that actual performance again for many years afterwards. However, I always looked out for them. I made an effort to watch any old archived repeat shows of live music from around that period on the off-chance but with no luck.

The band was afterwards largely forgotten, but not by me. I bought the single as soon as I found it. I liked it, but I was obviously a little biased. It was a little disappointing that there was no picture of her on the cover but at least I could hear her voice in there, continuing to make me feel warm even years later. I remember driving around with the CD in my car thinking "There will be no one else playing this CD now." That made me feel quite unique. In the CD notes, there were few details about the members of the band. I didn't even know her name. She had naturally beautiful dark hair and eyes. She wore large earrings that swung with her every movement including each smile. Everything about her was completely natural. Her smiling eyes, her hair, mouth and that especially unusual complexion were all as Mother Nature bestowed upon her. Everything was right. I knew that she would be like that all the time. Those eyes! I think that for any of us, be us men or women, we only perhaps get a feeling like that a couple of times in our lifetimes.

Finding out more about this particular girl was not an easy job. Only the band name, songwriter and the producer were ever credited to the recording. Researching anything was never easy in those days. Those were the days before much information had been available on the Internet. It took a lot of time and effort. Then, whenever I did find any information about the band from a new source, I just found that it was just a re-wording of information given in their original press release. The group apparently had returned unsuccessfully to Wellington and disbanded shortly afterwards. I hit a brick wall with my search so lost my enthusiasm for it.

It wasn't until 2006, ironically ten summers later, when I decided to look for her again. Then I began to make breakthroughs. I was prompted into action when an idle keyword search in a quiet lunchtime showed that someone had uploaded a rather grainy VHS recording of that TV performance up to the Internet in one of those video-sharing sites and there were comments discussing the performance. I then saw that performance for only the second time in my life. I was amazed that it was exactly how I remembered it. Nothing was any different. Every sound and every move she made were how I had them stored in my memory. The girl was again completely stunning. I knew she would be. She moved again in a perfect way. By then, the newly available powerful web search engines began to make my detective work easier. I only wished technology like that had been available to me ten years before.

Some years earlier I had moved into the music business myself by developing my own sampling software. My product had begun to sell well. I knew the product itself would have a finite lifespan but for the first time in my life I was able to have a high standard of living. A relative had also left me a rather large bequest in a will. I took some time away from my offices and had money to spend. By then I also had growing connections in the music business including a few overseas. When I was given the chance to work abroad, I took it instantly. New Zealand would be very nice. I knew that trends in technology, like the artists, in the music business, were never around for long so I decided to take the opportunity while I could.

I decided to treat my trip as a chance to do a little work promoting the installation of my software, do a little sight-seeing and would do a little personal research while I was there.

Her name and last known location took just three phone calls and three days. I began to get nervous for the first time when I began to repeat her name in my head. I wasn't sure of the pronunciation. Fortunately for me she was still singing. I then had an excuse to have contact. With my success and connections came a new social confidence and even though at the time I was occasionally rubbing shoulders with stars, I still felt butterflies as my detective work began to close in on the object of my affections.

She was quite young, only about twenty apparently, when working as a session vocalist, she was asked to guest on that song. That explained why her name was never on the credits of the original song. Then it struck me that I could not be sure then that this particular girl was the same girl who danced on the TV performance. Maybe that was only a dancer hired in the UK. Was I chasing someone who did not exist?

I realised that she would have been about thirty by then. As I began to travel around various studios and talk to various contacts "in the know" I soon found out that she was still based in Wellington. A later phone call tipped me off where she was assisting on a new album and I made arrangements to fit in that particular studio to my schedule in order to "have a look at their equipment" and generally loiter as I masqueraded under some excuse that I could improve some of their sound quality.

The producer was fairly laid back and did not even notice that I was around. I arrived there a couple of hours before she was due for her session. That was a mistake and only added to my nervousness even more.

Only when a door opened behind me and two otherwise unrecognisable formless soaking figures in raincoats arrived that I truly knew I had made the right move. Raincoats were removed and hair rubbed. Of course I went bright red and turned to bury my head into a thick manual. The vocalists dried themselves and chatted in English before making themselves coffee while reading lyric sheets.

She was probably even nicer in real life than I had ever imagined. Little could she have ever known of the reason why I was there in that very room with her that day. I had finally made it. It had all been worthwhile, even to get this far. What an achievement. Actually it is sometimes kind of worrying how easy it is to track people down these days using the Internet. She wore a lot of make up and was much shorter than I imagined but she was so, so very perfect. The two singers smelled lovely.

Without catching her eye or being obvious, I began to survey her. It was good news at least that there was no wedding or engagement ring.

I spent time actually shaking while I watched her performing her lines. Fortunately neither she nor anyone else seemed to notice how intently I must have been staring at her. I just could not believe I was actually there, in front of her.

Then came the chance for a chat when we all hurried across the rain-splattered road to a bar for lunch. This lasted for about two hours and involved lots of alcohol paid for by the singer's manager. Unfortunately I was pinned into a corner seat near the back of the large table and I could not get near my target. I ended up sitting close to the other session singer. I told her how good they were sounding that day and began tentatively to turn the questions towards her friend.

"Do you know if is she is….er…attached?" I asked, trying unconvincingly to sound casual.

"Oh, yes. She has lived with her girlfriend for years."

Well that was that, I supposed. I could move on.

I'm glad that I went anyway. "Better to have loved………" as they say.

One of my customers in Wellington was producing an up-and-coming young singer called Cristina. I ended up working with her and spending the whole summer there. We married last year.

And …she is just perfect.

Steve Morris

"If only..."

I remember it was one of those miserable murky nights in December. The only thing that stops people becoming any more miserable than they already are at that time of year is the thought of Christmas. Then, when that is all over with; it is back to the murk until spring. One of these years I'm going to hibernate right through.

Anyway, I was driving home on a Friday night in rush hour. It had been dark all day long and it had never stopped raining.

The guy on the radio said "If I was Mother Nature, I wouldn't have even bothered opening for business today. I'd have written this one off and moved straight to Saturday."

The car was a cosy little cocoon and I was having a take away Balti later that night with a mate. At least the traffic was moving. The heater was on full and I was toasting away nicely.

Then I noticed her. By the roadside, a young lady was standing by her car, looking soaking wet and pretty helpless. Holding her anorak over her head with both hands staring into the open car bonnet, she still looked very attractive even in her helpless way. She wasn't deliberately trying to flag down drivers but I could tell from her body language that she was desperate for one of us to stop to help. Rather than feel sorry for her, to me she looked striking. She was a welcome sparkle shining in that wretched gloom. I slowed. I was getting close. The young lady squinted at me through the starry blur of my car windscreen, her face wrinkled against Mother Nature's icy hosepipe. She probably couldn't see past my headlights and wipers. Rain was now streaming down both sides of the road. It was a filthy night.

I thought I had better stop. It *was* nearly Xmas.

My car was now a little bakery. The fan heater was blowing warm air up my trouser legs. I felt it rustling against the hairs. My team's manager was for once doing a rare frank interview on the radio. Tomorrow was a big match.

Now that I was level with the damsel in distress, it was decision time.

I could see more. She was dressed in a lavender dress. She obviously had no intention of being outside that night. The dress was totally inappropriate for the weather and the reflection of the yellow street lamps emphasised the soaked material. I liked that. Not just because she was drenched and the dress hugged her figure transparently. It was because so many young women those days dressed like men, in jeans and pullovers. She did look really nice. I began to wonder about her life and who she was. I wondered if she had a family. I wondered where she was going that night. Where was her partner? She had such a remarkable face with just that lovely bone structure that made her a natural beauty. I would remember it.

I drove past.

I was sure that the breakdown lorry would arrive soon and the interview was getting heated on the radio. By then, it was also hot in my car. That was where I intended staying and so I pressed my right foot down.

I went home and had my laddish Balti with my mate who I saw every Friday night.

"Could have been a good opportunity missed." He remarked as he always did with a full mouth of curry when I told him of the drive home that night. Women were a fairly common topic of conversation. We were both senior authorities on the matter and we were both perennially single.

He might have been right. It was so difficult to meet a nice girl those days. For me, approaching them was always a problem. I never had a lot of confidence. I always felt clichéd and uncomfortable talking to them in bars. I always felt I came across as desperate and a slob. That night would have been a good excuse for me. I wished that I had stopped. I thought that if I had stopped, then maybe it could have been a beginning. Who knows?

I did think about her often afterwards or at least of her image. In all probability she would have been already married with several kids and a whole package of undesirable baggage. Yet she became some ideal woman who would remain in my mind. She became a woman besides whom I would measure and compare all the other women that I would meet. And there would be quite a few in my tedious trawl through bachelorhood.

I found myself conjuring up an image of my ideal woman then when I met other women; saying to myself "She wouldn't do that because she is a class above you." I even gave her a name. I called her Miranda, which was my favourite name at the time. Rather than lament a missed opportunity, I resolved that one day I would meet another Miranda, I would come to her rescue, she would be a wonderful person, and life would be pretty good. Simple.

She was out there. I needed a wife but I needed a wife like Miranda.

That became more and more apparent as my friends got married one by one and left me to live my own single life. As it happened, I never did get married and time moved on and on. Curries on Friday night were never meant to be a permanent thing.

I became cynical again. Where do you meet nice women like that? I had the conversation countless times over a Vindaloo.

One Saturday, some years later, while filling up at the local petrol station, I bumped into Andy.

Andy and I were very close friends when we were young. We went through our teenage years together then went our separate ways to different colleges. It was great to see him again. Pushed for time at the filling station, we exchanged phone numbers.

He rang me at the weekend and invited me for dinner at his place.

Andy had done well for himself. He was one of those "well-rounded" people who are always going to do well. He had not just done well financially but I could see that he was genuinely contented with his lot. He was happy. I was happy for him. It made a change to see someone in that position. It seemed obvious that one of the main reasons for his good fortune was his family. He had a teenager called Robert who was the spitting image of his dad and just as well rounded. He had a nice home far away from the hustle of town. The most valuable part of his life, however, was his wife Serena. She was lovely. Actually, she was magnificent. She was exactly what a wife should be. I won't go into details now.

In fact, I will. Serena glowed. Serena shone. Serena was a teacher. She was intelligent, talented, wholesome and devoted to her family. I am sure that Serena could cope with anything life threw at her and would still come out smiling. I wasn't worthy of someone like Serena. I know I promised not to go into details. I can't keep this one to myself.

However, I didn't fancy her. No. That would have been wrong. It would have been wrong to become a predatory male in that fine example of a family. We need families like that.

The conversation eventually moved on to my own circumstances. They expressed surprise that I lived on my own. Perhaps they were just being polite. I must come across as being a bit of a slob sometimes. I moaned about my loneliness and the lack of real opportunities to meet a nice wife.

"So how did you guys meet?"

Serena was first to answer.

"Well, one Friday night on the way to a Christmas party, my car broke down...."

"It's an ill wind"

"Yes. It was going back nearly seventy five years, but I can still remember that time quite vividly." Said the old guy shaking his head. "It was winter 2011 when we first noticed we had big problems. Oh yes, I remember it all..."

I was interviewing the pensioner as part of my college research project on climate trends. As with all men his age, his eyes widened with enthusiasm when he found someone willing to listen to his memories. My job was to sort out his facts from his fiction.

"Even back then, winters weren't what they used to be. My own grandfather used to tell me that he could actually remember when there was snowfall over Christmas time. Every year."

I remembered some old Christmas cards someone once showed me. The old guy went on:

"The fun and games started with a really hot summer. Temperatures were breaking records all over the place. We had no need to fly to the Costa on holiday! That was fine with us kids. It was a long, sunny vacation and we had some damned good fun as you do when you are young. When we got ready to go back to school in September however, it was still hot and lessons felt just the same as if we were in summer term. We didn't need our blazers or jumpers. Then October arrived and it was still ridiculously warm. By then at least it had started to rain a little again. Grass seemed to be growing as fast as ever and hanging baskets were still freely flowering. In October! The leaves on the trees showed no signs whatsoever of changing colour and the arrival of the oncoming autumn was nowhere to be seen. I took notice of all that kind of thing because my parents owned and ran a garden centre. So weather played a big part in our daily routines.

We always had a family of house martins who lived in the roof of our house. Or maybe we lived in their house. Every year they would migrate a few thousand miles from the South of France to our eaves with intentions of disturbing our sleep and pooping on our car. Before the autumn weather arrived and well ahead of any weather forecaster, they would begin their long journey back south before returning each following spring. That particular year we noticed that they were still hanging around weeks after their normal departure date. Also, I remember my father when he accidentally drove over some baby rabbits on the way to work. "Don't we usually play chicken with these in the spring, dad?" I remember asking him. Things were wrong. Confused by the mild weather, the animals didn't know quite literally, if they were coming or going.

The mild nights drew in. It was very odd. Kids came trick-or-treating without wearing any coats. Those that wore costumes were sweating uncomfortably inside them. It was going dark at the proper time but the air itself didn't feel right at all. The wind had not changed direction and was still blowing a warm current up from the south. The press began to make light of the situation. Photos were taken of a Guy Fawkes effigy sat on a beach in Bermuda shorts. Everywhere, people were taking advantage of the Mother Nature's seasonal "bonus" of 2011.

Autumn Sundays were still a good day to go for a family day-out even in late-November. I remember seeing people sitting outside our local pub in the beer garden one afternoon. It was surreal. At that point people were happy to enjoy it, rather than think anything more sinister about it. No one seemed unduly concerned. "Don't worry. Winter will arrive with a bang soon." Everyone said.

Well, it didn't.

Winter never came.

Shortly after Christmas, kids at school started dropping like flies with gastric viruses. My class was only half-full some weeks. Everywhere businesses were short-staffed due to illness. The doctors said that frosts were needed to help kill the airborne germs.

Well, the frosts didn't come.

Freakish thunderstorms began to horsewhip the UK and short sharp bursts of very heavy rain battered our gardens into submission at least once a week. The press labelled them the first "British Monsoons".

As in many adverse situations, some people did very well out of it. Air conditioning equipment, refrigerators, electric fans and even convertible cars all began to sell particularly well. The public weren't complaining. People spent the cash they would have spent on winter fuel on other things.

My father even tried to cash in by importing lots of outdoor tropical plants for the garden centre. He suggested that they could be grown outside all winter, if things stayed as they were.

"Well, it's an ill wind." he said.

It was not all good news. At that point farmers were reporting big problems with lambing. There was also a problem with milk production. The cows just didn't feel like the job. They didn't know where they were. Now, the crops were failing and food prices were on the way up. People didn't like that.

We didn't notice the spring bulbs coming up in February. Snowdrops and crocuses had all been up since November and now looked stretched and confused. The trees all looked pale and tired. Their leaves were by then anaemic.

People were going around in shorts and t-shirts again by March. You'd have thought they would be happy about that considering how we grumbled about our long British winter.

Well, they weren't because by then certain food prices were rocketing out of control and everyone seemed to be miserable with their constant colds and stomach viruses. People were permanently irritable. We had too much of a good thing. Trouble was beginning to spontaneously appear on the streets of towns and cities as tempers flared.

As every young child should know, being let loose inside a sweet shop is a wonderful thing to happen. However, there is only a finite amount of sweets and chocolate one can eat before things begin to go wrong, the whole novelty wears off, and sweet things become distasteful. People became fraught, tense and irritable. Driving a car was altogether unpleasant and often dangerous. Road rage was everywhere by late spring as people sat in steaming traffic jams. Police cars carried bottled water. The UK was not a happy place and for the first time ever, people began to dread the rest of the summer ahead.

The landscape of the UK itself was changing. Many old established native trees had died over the "winter". The younger ones had lean, leggy and bloodless growth where this year's soft wood had grown from last year's soft wood. The branches still contained last season's shrivelled leaves that had not frozen and dropped without our usual abrasive winter winds. The fish stocks in the North Sea were at critical levels due to warm water currents. Following these, dolphins and sharks were now making fairly regular appearances off the beaches of even Northern seaside resorts. All manner of confused exotic jellyfish were stinging bathers.

The Governments decided to act. Coal-fired power stations were closed down, electricity rationed and carbon-based fuels began to be taxed extortionately. Unnecessary road travel was discouraged. Our only chance was to immediately cut the amount of damaging emissions. We had no choice. The politicians decided that whatever short-term damage we might do to the economy may be nothing compared to our long-term life prospects. Emergency legislation was rushed through Parliament. Only Mother Nature would ultimately decide if our efforts were to be too little too late. People, because they could see the damaging evidence with their own eyes surprisingly went along with the newly imposed emergency laws. Individuals found flouting the laws were pilloried publicly as enemies of our climate.

We then had another two thoroughly unpleasant summers and uncomfortably mild winters. Learning to adapt was all we could do as our lifestyles began to resemble that of Mediterranean people.

The British had always been renowned for their small talk of weather. It was amazing just how more obsessed than ever people became with that very subject. Weather forecasts, especially the long-range ones, became a national obsession. Rumours of oncoming major changes in wind direction or air pressure often spread mouth-to-mouth in supermarkets and workplaces. Trade in gambling on weather became big business. In November 2014, on the night of that desperately welcome frost, there were street parties in some places.

It was like the end of the war. The job wasn't complete. We all knew that we would have to work hard to keep the peace..."

I began to type up the interview.

"Real snow at Christmas? No... he made that one up."

"Let the good times roll"

"And you said this guy went just the same way?"

"Yes, he just went nuts with a machete around the shopping mall last night. It is amazing he didn't get any more people with that thing."

"So he's another one then"

"Oh yes…He keeps saying 'I just had to.' That is his only reason"

"Why, I wonder…Why?"

And so the conversation went between the two dismayed detectives. They weren't used to this. After having such an easy time at work in the last few years, policemen like these simply couldn't cope with the growing number of these seemingly motiveless and unconnected crimes cropping up randomly around the country. The USA was becoming a dangerous place to live once more. We all thought those days were behind us. Things were changing.

Thirty years ago, depression had become a big problem in the USA. The total cost to the taxpayer in terms of healthcare, the economy and absent days from work was huge. Rather than just accept the natural polarity that some people were fully contented with their lives while other people felt thoroughly miserable about theirs, medical scientists tried to do something once-and-for-all about it.

They eventually devised a simple, safe and stable solution to treat the problem permanently. It was found that severely depressed people were missing an essential brain chemical. Previously medication had to be given regularly to stimulate its production. The drug had to be taken regularly and reliably, there were side effects and it only worked for some of the patients. The new solution to all of this was a one-off insertion of a tiny microchip into the brain designed to release an exact timed dose of the crucial missing chemical. There were no unpleasant side effects. There were no diet or alcohol restrictions. There was no addiction. People could go into hospital, have their painless operation, forget about it and the clouds would soon lift. It was as simple as that. It was to be a conveyor belt type of system with hundreds of patients having their operations each day. Everyone would be happy, quite literally.

Rigorous trials took place on volunteers for five years. They were a profound success. The drug did not interact with any other medications. The quality of the volunteers' lives improved dramatically. The patients felt literally warm, sunny, energetic and happy each and every day without feeling cloudy or sedated. They jumped quickly out of bed each morning and looked forward to the day ahead rather than dreading it.

"Look at his background. Just a regular guy like the others. Steady job with no personal problems."

"Yes. These people have no reason for it. They just go pop somehow."

"Fourth this week. The guy with the truck has been the worst so far after what he did. He was a granddad. You know the chief is stepping up patrols from Friday?"

"Yeah... He's making sure there is one of us standing around each Wall Mart and he wants two guys on each main road in rush hour. It can't just be the heat this year. It is nothing like last year's summer."

The operation eventually became available by doctors' prescriptions. At first it was only prescribed to the most serious cases but as time went on it was made more generally available. It certainly improved the quality of many people's lives. It took about five weeks to work then people began to gradually behave differently. It was referred to as the "op" rather than "a serotonin management implantation." Soon, people without any history of depression were asking for the operation in case they developed it in later life. The Government drew the line at anyone under 21 having the operation unless there was a serious need for it.

The patients began to take life less seriously. They saw positives in everything, some for the very first time in their lives. People who would usually complain about the heat or streaming hay fever would deliberately take a detour through the park each morning before work just to keep an eye on how new flowers were doing, no matter how much their noses were running. Those people who would normally sit and fume in congested traffic would take their favourite CDs on a long route to work just to sing along in the tailback. People began to live life to the full, filling their time with pleasurable things. It was as if they were making up for lost time. Everyone became charitable. Everyone became friendly. Religious attendances of all persuasions grew significantly as did marriages. The birth rates increased dramatically. The politicians were pleased. There was less crime. It was a bit like the "summer of love" all over again but without that music or pot. People of all ages and lifestyles were involved.

"The machete guy just keeps yelling. "I needed to". What's all that about?" One of the detectives said to the other peering through the barred window of the police cell.

"I heard him. He seemed at first to think he'd get some sort of relief from it. He hasn't. He's just as crazy now."

People were becoming literally bored with feeling happy each and every day. The feeling of happiness was losing its effect on people's minds because people never felt sad. They needed to feel sad occasionally to be able to compare the feeling of happiness.

To fully appreciate how warm a fireside is, you have to feel cold and wet beforehand. Food always tastes at its best when we are very hungry before we eat it. In the same way, because people had become permanently happy, in the long-term they needed something else to make them feel the real benefit of their happiness. They needed unhappiness to balance their lives. They needed anger to balance with their calm. Over the years, they had become immune to the feeling of pleasure.

There were becoming a lot of emerging incidents of rage, pent-up frustration and anger. People had to blow up. Innocent people were becoming hurt.

The scientists finally admitted that they had got it wrong. They worked on a solution.

The hospitals would soon become fully booked for reversal procedures. It would cost the Government an absolute fortune.

In the meantime, a lot more policemen would be needed.

Steve Morris

"Memories are made of this"

It had always been a well-known fact that, for some reason, we only use a small percentage of our brain's capacity. We had never known what large parts of our brain were actually used for. It had mystified scientists for many years. That was, until a chance discovery made by some Japanese scientists.

They found, by a complete accident, that the brain was really one very sophisticated video recorder. It was a sort of hard drive containing a lifetime of photographed memories.

Our eyes were taking a series of snapshots at regular intervals during every hour of every day of our lives. They were storing them as electronic neuron-data through our entire existence. The reason why Mother Nature wanted our brain to do this is still, to this day, entirely unknown. I suppose we will never know why. Also the means by which the images could be viewed naturally was not yet discovered.

They were discovered purely by accident by two scientists in a Tokyo university doing research into sleep therapy. They were measuring the electronic impulses of brain waves during volunteers' sleeping sessions. Interference into some of their sensitive electronic monitoring equipment was accidentally converted into direct monochrome images.

As soon as people heard that the technology was available for people to view their own past memories, obviously everyone wanted to see their own.

Imagine if you could watch your own long-lost priceless childhood memories on TV. You could see in detail all those images where you never had a camera at hand at the time. People imagined what it would be like to see the smiling face of a long-gone relative.

However, the service was only to be made available to the very rich as the technology was very expensive. The processing of the images was time-consuming and there was only two devices functioning correctly so far in the world. It was a little like how at one-time, those commercial flights into space were chartered only by rock stars and business tycoons.

The police became immediately interested in the technology because they could ascertain exactly what crime witnesses saw. The technology was used in court in a few very high profile cases at the time to convince witnesses to change their version of events. They hoped to make the images legally admissible as evidence.

Interestingly, to add to the nostalgia of the video memories, they were all projected as black-and-white images on the screens. We indeed did think in black-and-white after all.

The eldest residents of the USA were invited to have their memories recorded for free so as to preserve images of actual events for historical interest.

The fortunate senior citizens were fascinated with viewing their own memories but were cautious of other people viewing them and they were often disappointed with the results. Those summers seemed not quite as sunny as they remembered. Those seas were not quite so still and those girls at school were actually not quite so pretty. We all soon began to realise how our own memories become exaggerated over time.

One old guy commented on how good his eyesight was back then and said that it was like watching a fantasy film. Like others, he disputed some of the memories. We assumed he was denying some of the unsavoury images, out of sheer embarrassment.

Like some silent film, to add to the atmosphere there was still no sound to accompany the images but the scientists were working on that.

After the viewings of several people the equipment needed tweaking, as the development of images was proving too slow a process. Keen to exploit a commercial opportunity, the Japanese wanted to develop a quick and efficient way of bottling and selling this commodity.

The US president lay down for his recording session. The eager scientists around him talked him through the painless procedure. This was a major coup for them. With the approval and publicity of as big a client as the US President, the sky would be the limit as regards sales of this technology. The sensors were fitted to the lobes of his head and the scientists gave instructions as to how to relax. After twenty minutes, images began to be produced and recording of the scenes began. Images of the president's childhood soon began to appear.

One particular episode of his college days seemed to convey many images. The president was seen to be at a party and was quite clearly smoking dope. His advisors were quick to point out that although every student was doing this at the time, this would have to be edited out of any images that went public.

The president and his fellow students were seen to be relaxing after the party by a log fire. At one unexpected point a large eagle entered the room. It was much bigger than the men. It swooped upon one of the students, picked him up and flew out of the open door.

The scientists looked at each other.

The president began to sweat.

The president grinned.

One by one, the giant eagle returned to carry off each member of the party. Finally the president was carried off and deposited in an endless warm sea of cotton wool

The fault was apparent. ...

The device was replaying dreams, not memories.

"Potential Energy"

According to reports, from across the street, the woman had seen her toddler become trapped under the wheels of a car. With just one arm she lifted up the car while with the other, she pulled the toddler from underneath. It was as simple as that. She was just an ordinary woman and afterwards had no idea how she managed it.

Urban myths or not, we've all heard stories like this one before. But it couldn't actually be true....

Over the years and perhaps without realising quite how many, I had heard numerous anecdotes like that one. It seemed that when in absolute desperation, ordinary people could be capable of some pretty fantastic feats of strength. Like our glossy comic-book heroes, from somewhere deep within they can find the power to get themselves through near-impossible life-or-death situations.

Around the time that particular story was in the headlines, I was working as a scientist mainly involved in performance enhancing nutrition research for the armed forces. I often daydreamed of discovering a miracle supplement by using the very chemicals that exist already within our bodies. I planned to bottle it, sell it and it would make me a fortune. Simple. But it had to be something completely natural. It had to be something that would never do any harm. There had been enough of that in recent years. The right chemical was out there. I knew it. I just had to find it before anyone else did.

However, discovering any drug more effective than those already available proved to be difficult. It was a laborious chore. Waiting tediously for the results of side-effect trials on volunteers was an agonisingly slow process.

The story of the car-lifting woman made me think. If the chemical answers were already there inside the body, then there would be no need to worry about side effects. My job was to find the chemical trigger.

I discussed my ideas with Trevor, a fellow researcher on the project, and we decided to investigate. We got a little funding to help with the study.

We agreed that the first thing to do was to look at what went on inside blood during extreme situations. We needed to find out what actually made the body behave differently at that time. We had to simulate an incident.

Oddly, our search began by us visiting a man who kept dogs. He kept English Bull Terriers for dubious purposes, if you understand my meaning. Bull terriers are normally quite gentle creatures around people. When angered, however, they can unleash bursts of explosive aggression towards other animals. Sadly, this had meant their cruel use in sport for as long as they have been around. Their tenacity is quite unlike any other dog and they are born fighting-machines. I was convinced they would be full of all sorts of hormones and chemicals when they were in full flow.

Trevor and I took blood samples of one of the dogs then watched while the handler sadistically and unpleasantly "wound up" the caged animal until he was into frenzy. The dog's eyes glazed over. Hot steam-like breath and foam fizzed out of his muzzle. At this point we took blood samples again. When the cage door opened, it took the three of us to hold the dog down, and we really struggled.

After the blood analysis we were none the wiser. Apart from the stress hormones and adrenaline chemicals that we already knew about, we did not get much further.

Animal research was one thing but the end product was for use by humans. We needed data from people. Here, research was going to be difficult as simulating the necessary situation was not really on. We had to wait.

While we were working on our respective research projects, Trevor and I monitored the news headlines closely over the next year or two in search of some potential heroes. We tried to interview and test anyone who claimed that they'd had one of these super-human experiences. Of course, we were always too late arriving after the event for our tests to be of any use. The necessary wonder-chemical had, by then, dissipated back to where it came leaving no trace. We got on with our lives, but kept a close eye on the news.

Our work took us to Italy at one point. We interviewed an American soldier who had saved some civilians. They had all been travelling home on a bus late one night when the vehicle left the road. Probably being driven too quickly it suffered a tyre blow-out when rounding a bend. It broke through a safety barrier and plummeted into a lake leaving the 21 occupants trapped inside the coach in icy water. This particular soldier had managed to break through the glass and had somehow dragged the passengers individually and even in pairs to safety. The story understandably hit the front pages fairly quickly and the soldier became an overnight celebrity. We got there soon afterwards and interviewed and examined the soldier closely. We were told that strangely, in the nearby American military base, the equipment used to routinely measure radiation levels had detected some brief strange readings that night around the time of the event. We were surprised that we got hold of that information.

Obviously the military regularly use this sensitive equipment so as to detect possible nuclear, biological and chemical attacks on their bases.

His blood contained slightly elevated levels of radioactivity but levels were quickly returning to normal. If we had arrived any later we would have missed this. So we tested a sample of other personnel around the base. Their levels were normal.

There were some other interestingly similar cases around the globe but the next incident was to prove the most significant and we were close to hand.

Our work took us over to the conflict zone in Iraq. This was something we were not looking forward to but we had a stroke of luck. By sheer chance we were near the next significant flashpoint event. Sadly, events like this *were* probably more than likely to occur in Iraq if they were to occur anywhere.

The events unfolded at a building that was being used as a temporary hospital near Basra. A car bomb had set the place on fire horrifically and hundreds of patients and medical staff were trapped inside. The roof of the unsuitable building collapsed under the stress of the inferno and many people were literally being cremated alive. An Iraqi civilian, who was about to visit two of his family members having treatment there, realised that he had to act quickly. Bursting through the emergency services and military cordons by literally tossing people out of the way, he began to tear at the molten framework of the building with his bare hands. Seemingly free from any pain, he ripped through wooden beams and tossed aside lumps of concrete and brick as if they were cardboard and polystyrene. Minutes later he was carrying out patients including two of his family. Needless to say he soon collapsed and needed some prompt serious medical treatment himself.

Trevor quickly disappeared amongst the military with his questions while I carried out physical tests on this real-life hero. His injuries were bizarrely minimal and he would survive unscathed. His radioactivity levels, however, were elevated considerably. Of course he had no knowledge of how he actually had managed this rescue act. In fact he remembered very little at all after the event.

The next morning, when I had finished interviewing him and the tests were all done I sought out my companion. He had spent most of the night in discussions with military officials. Things were different that morning. Not just with Trevor, but everything seemed simply different.

I found him sitting with his back against a wall staring out into an unkempt gravel field of yellow weeds. His eyes were glossy as he played with some stalks of grass between his fingers.

Trevor was calm and silent but Trevor was very tearful. I had known him a long time. He was not usually like this. These were the kind of tears one sheds only once or twice in a lifetime.

I eventually got some sense out of him. Afterwards, we both sat quietly for a very long time.

That conversation, as I can remember, went something like this:

"So, let me get this right what you are telling me, this radiation burst which they detected must have come from above. Is that what you are saying?"

"Yes…."

"And it could only have arrived as a narrow beam right into the very individual in question?"

"Yes…."

"What is the probability that the individual could have been hit randomly?"

"Next to nothing."

"So it was aimed directly at him?"

"Without a doubt………."

"The Remainder"

"I had always wanted to run my own company. I had always wanted a big successful company. And we couldn't get much bigger that Holden Securities now could we?"

I smiled as I interviewed this young hotshot developer. I liked him. He was sharp, logical and keen with just a little bit of mischief about him. His background was in programming, much like my own. He understood raw code just like myself. I was going to give him a job but he would have to work harder in the interview. I like to see them under a little pressure to see what they are made of. I decided to make him sweat for a while I bragged a little more about my company's achievements.

"I don't even know how much we are worth at the moment. The company is worth millions. Heaven knows what the next accounts will say. Pretty much everyone is using Holden Securities' software at the moment."

That was no exaggeration.

"I'm going to sell it soon and retire."

This last thought I said to myself.

"Welcome on board Warren" I said to him finally after his prolonged grilling. He had done well. He would be a good employee. I liked this kid.

It all began about thirty years ago. Straight from college I got a job with one of the high street banks and started to work in their credit card department. The job was easy for me and I had time on my hands, so I had the opportunity to observe our customers' lives. I learned a lot about their spending habits.

Do you know how many people get charged interest on their credit cards every month of the year? Do you know how much they pay in interest when it is all added together? "Most people" and "a total of millions of pounds" are the answers.

You see, we didn't need customers who paid off their balances every month.

I found computer programming easy and soon got a job working on the code for the calculation of interest charges on people's statements. I soon spotted it. The crime was a simple one. Calculation of interest was a pretty basic one of multiplication with sometimes a division for instalments. This often did not end up with an exact figure of pounds and pence. Sometimes there was a tiny amount left over such as £23.4525. I managed to alter the code so the decimal pence figure was rounded down and the tiny remainder credited electronically to a secret account. The amounts were admittedly very small. However with so many people borrowing on their credit cards at that time often way above their means, the little amounts soon began to add together. After a year or two there was quite a balance. I had to then start emptying it regularly. The point was that it was not a crime really. Half pennies had been abolished so we can forget that. No one would miss the tiny remainders smaller than half a pence. It was waste money. It was wood shavings. Nobody would lose out. So it was not a crime.

Three years later and at the time I left the bank, my little nest egg had grown into around sixty five thousand pounds. I hadn't touched it but that was about to change.

I decided to use the money to set up my own company and, if anyone did ever ask, I told them that I had inherited the money from an old aunt.

With my flair for programming and with a bit of luck on my side, it soon started to make a modest profit especially as electronic commerce leapt in popularity.

The company began to grow and our reputation soon gained strength built around the success of our financial security software. I think this was partly because of my policy to employ people in senior positions who had, shall we say, rather shady backgrounds in financial areas. People like that knew how criminal minds might work. They were particularly appreciative of me because often no one else would ever employ them. I gave them a chance and they rewarded me with hard work. I let them know straight from the start that I was always one step ahead of them if they ever fancied a little pilfering from my company!

On and on we went, each year's success improved on the last. We even got a "Queen's award" for export a couple of years ago. It was a good job she didn't have a thumb through my employee list. Holden Securities was now pretty huge and it was all down to my hard work and a little luck. Overall it had all worked out well considering my modest early days of a naïve teenager working in the bank.

Warren started work quietly in the company but soon began to show a lot of flair. I could see his talent and I took him on as a personal project. Under my wing and that of my colleagues, he soon became a very talented programmer. We all took to Warren. I spent a lot of extra time with him, grooming him to take over a senior position in the company without actually telling him. In many ways, to me he fitted the image of the son I had never had.

We all began work on our latest project of making some headway in the emerging Asian markets. The plan was for me to sell up in just a few months. I had begun secret discussions with a buyer. Holden Securities was then bigger than it had ever been. I was made for life. No problem.

I had never before lost an employee to a head-hunter. What was all this about? I had certainly never had an employee poached. Most ironic of all, Warren was poached by an agency working on behalf of the same high street bank where I had first started to work. This annoyed me.

I was annoyed because of the time we had invested in him, showing him a few "tricks" he would certainly never learn elsewhere, I am sure. At his age, I suppose he was hot property. Most of all, due to my fondness of Warren and his exceptional talents, I took it personally.

Still, life went on. Why should I have worried? I was selling up in a couple of months. I was getting married. I couldn't even be bothered pursuing the bank for compensation for the loss of Warren.

It was a Tuesday afternoon when investigators visited me about a case of "embezzlement" which had taken place in a high street bank some thirty years ago. Apparently some recently recruited hotshot programmer called Warren unearthed it.

As I sit awaiting trial, I curse the day I employed that kid.

"Voices"

I was hearing voices.

They came as I drifted off to sleep. At first I only used to remember them half way through the following day and then I could only remember odd snippets of what was actually said. I was definitely hearing voices.

Life was very busy for me. I worked hard at my job, enjoyed life and lived it to the full. Bed was a place to sleep. So when I finally made it to bed I was tired and I usually fell asleep quickly. It never took me long to drop off. Then, as I slid along that soft, smooth, warm passageway between sleepiness and sleep, I was in the brief company of the voices. Each and every night it happened. I could tell what they were saying at the very moment they were speaking. They were talking in plain English. However, they were talking to each other and not to me.

I told my friends and colleagues about them. Some people advised me to see a psychiatrist. That was usually the thing to suggest to someone complaining about the "voices" in their head. Other people told me that I had been "working far too hard recently" or that I had "spent too long living on my own after the divorce." Well, maybe they were right about the work. They could stuff the psychiatrist.

One thing I was certain about however was that the voices were real.

For as long as I could remember these bedtime dialogues had been with me. Like tuning in to a reliably scheduled TV soap, they occurred reliably at the same time every night. I generally forgot about them in the mornings as I woke in my usual late rush to face the hectic day ahead.

I had heard those anecdotes of people who could receive harmonics from radio stations through the amalgam fillings in their teeth. Well, I did not have any of those, so I could rule that one out.

I was certainly not dreaming it. Dreams were different than these. I was half awake every time. These were real.

At the weekend I made the effort to get the bottom of it. My rural house was very quietly located with no neighbours within earshot. There was never a lot of background noise. I could find no radios or TVs left on unintentionally. At all other times there was complete silence in the bedroom apart from the odd agricultural vehicle using the country road nearby. The dog slept lightly at night on the landing. He was sensitive to any noise near to the house.

This had all been going on too long. In my work, I was the sort of guy who liked to get things "done" and out of the way. I decided to somehow record the conversations, find out what they were all about and find out who was speaking them.

I left a tape recorder working by my bedside all night to see if that picked up any sounds while I was asleep. Well, it didn't. So the voices had to be inside my head.

In the morning, my memories of the conversations were always very vague. By definition of their timing, I wasn't at my most alert at the time of hearing them. I needed more than anything to find out the story behind them. They were beginning to annoy me and to affect my sleep.

I decided it would be a relief to get an exact transcript of what the voices were actually saying, word for word. I could remember the odd phrase that I was convinced was part of a topic of conversation. The words at first seemed diverse and unconnected as if they were chosen randomly out of some encyclopaedia. I began to compile a list: "projects.... doctor...fashion." They were neither speaking to me nor questioning me. Instead they seemed to be part of casual conversations between two or more people like those we all overhear while sitting opposite people on the train when you can only pick out occasional words. I was also convinced that the conversation was either repeating itself or continuing on from the previous night. Each episode was connected.

I decided I was in no position to accurately hand-write much at that time of night. After each snippet of conversation, it was always far too easy not to bother and to let my leaden head crash back onto the pillow until morning. I decided to try to wake myself immediately after each eavesdropped conversation and try to instantly repeat the words into the tape recorder before falling asleep. Then I could analyse them in the morning. I had to discipline myself into a routine of doing this each and every night from then on.

I was convinced each night that the voices themselves were speaking complete sense. There were always several sentences of dialogue at least. Maybe there was a few minutes' worth of chat. As I got into my routine, I found that when I lifted my head and spoke what I remembered into the tape recorder, I could only ever manage a few words at most.

As time went on, I slowly compiled a page full of words. I had to re-arrange them from their random order to make any sort of sense. There were many gaps of course between the key words in sentences, which I had to fill in as best I could, using my own words such as " I", "to", "and", and "as".

It took literally weeks to have enough words to make any kind of sense and months to form a whole conversation. Then I set about gradually putting the random jigsaw of sentences together. It was frustrating to keep it to myself but I wasn't going to get taken seriously by anyone until I had at least some workable dialogue.

One person, who I decided to name "friend one", seemed to lead the discussion. It sounded like a general conversation spoken in a relaxed manner like we all might have in the pub. They spoke of their lives and their work. Words such as "job", "tired", "time" and "late" occurred regularly. If anything, the conversation was not remarkable in any way. It could have belonged to anyone. I remembered that the voices were male but I could not recall their accents. I was not clear as to what they did for a living or whether they had wives and families.

As the words were gradually added to the dialogue, things took a chilling turn. I began to notice more unusual and concerning phrases coming from my "Friend One". The words "next generation permission" kept cropping up along side the words "child approval". They then also mentioned several times his impending "ceiling age". None of them ever mentioned their wives or partners.

Slowly, after many months of information gathering, and bewilderment from my colleagues, I had a couple of pages of speech. My "friends" were discussing their limited opportunities to produce offspring to the next generation before some time limit expired. Their government somehow defined this time limit. I suspected that this "time limit" was another word for their lifespan. I realised then that their lives were being talked of as some fixed-term contract as if there was a set limit of space in their "world". As people became old, their government could replace them with a child of which had to be pre-approved.

I became obsessed and fascinated with their lives the more I heard.

This telepathy had to really be from another world or from another time. As time went on, and with practice, I began to remember more words each morning. I continued to record them, and soon began to compile a large record of these eavesdropped dialogues. It was addictive and chilling.

One day my first friend said the most interesting thing so far.

He complained that when he was falling asleep at night, he was hearing voices.

"Winston Churchill"

Nothing.

The first thing that I remember was straining to open my eyes. Things were not right at all. My eyelids were of cast iron and the light blinding.

During the next few seconds I underwent my usual morning checking procedure: Where was I? What day was it? What was my first job of the day?

Then with a sunken feeling I remembered the previous night's accident. So that was why my head was spinning. I can distinctly remember the loud crack as a truck swerving wildly across the road thundered into my car.

It seems strange but comforting that I couldn't remember anything of events after that. No police. No hospital. No anything. My head was still gyrating but I felt, on the whole, that I couldn't have been hurt too badly. However, I couldn't remember the details of the previous night or how I got to bed.

"Can you hear me?"

A voice began speaking behind me. Or was it inside my head?

"Uh?" I replied as I tried to make sense of it.

It came again.

"Can you hear me?"

There was a figure leaning over the bed. I realised now that the bed was not my own.

I turned my head and squinted at the vague figure, my eyes still being burned by the blinding white light of the room. It was no one who I recognised.

He was tall, bald and middle-aged. He wore a one-piece uniform of white. He must have been a medic.

"Are you a doctor?" I asked, still not knowing quite which hospital they had taken me to.

"No. Are you Winston Churchill?"

I began to gain coherence and realised that there was no warm small talk.

"Are you crazy? Where am I?"

"Are you Winston Churchill?" He repeated in a monotone.

"Of course I am not Winston bloody Churchill! Now where am I?"

"Oh no. Not again. .....Who are you then?" groaned the 'doctor'

"Jacob Richardson," I replied

"Date of Birth? Place of birth?"

"First of December 1959. Cardiff"

Another 'doctor' appeared by the bed. The figure was strikingly similar to the first and the two seemed to engage in a private conversation.

"Excuse me." I began in a sarcastic rather than polite manner. "Will you please tell me which hospital this is and what is wrong with me exactly?" I pleaded as my head became clearer.

"We were looking for Winston Churchill."

"What do you mean 'looking for Winston Churchill'? He died 25 years ago."

I was beginning to get a little annoyed of this Winston Churchill rubbish. How long was I going to be in hospital? The doctor who was nearest to me smiled.

"About three thousand years ago actually"

"What?"

"He died around three thousand years ago. Look. A while ago we developed a clever little device that can transport the mind of any human who has ever lived into any body. You are the fifth person we have had out today. We wanted to talk to Winston Churchill today because we think it will be interesting."

This was all very silly. I moved my eyes downwards.

I looked at my body and was shocked to realise that I was not indeed in my own torso. Yet it felt like it was. I began to sweat. I could not move "my" body no matter how hard I tried. It was as if my limbs were not attached.

"What's wrong with my body? Whose body is this?" I demanded somewhat panic-stricken

"A scientist like ourselves," One of them replied.

He went on.

"You all seem quite surprised when we tell you that you died long ago in history. You can't seem to take it in. We do sympathise. We are sorry to have disturbed you but we had better get on with our work. We will put you back 'in' shortly."

"Disturbed me? Died? Put me back in where exactly?" I demanded.

This had all been rather a lot to take in but somehow at that point amazingly I was beginning to piece this paradox together and even come to terms with it.

These people, claiming to be from the far distant future had somehow discovered the science behind consciousness itself and had, for their recreation, been looking for a famous person to resurrect from my time and had mistakenly found me. These people were not from my future. I was from their past. I was a "nobody" found in error while searching for a celebrity.

"What year is this?" I had to ask.

"Er...In solar years 5012 or thereabouts. We do not very often use solar years as units like you did."

"So what is the world like now?" I astounded myself that I was beginning to believe everything they said and had many questions.

"Very different from the world you knew!" They both replied laughing.

At this point I noticed that their lips were not moving as they spoke yet their voices were clear in my mind. I thought I might be in fact dreaming it all but everything was so vivid.

"What will you do with me now? How long have I got?" I asked as I remembered the impending situation.

"10 minutes (in your units)" was the reply as the figures busied themselves pointing to various screens around the room, which resembled a TV studio more than a hospital room.

"Please put me back where I was," I asked politely but not really knowing why.

I was scared. I was scared of the unknown.

"Just a question...." I asked in a trembling voice. "While I am waiting."

"Earth. Is it at peace or war now?"

"Earth...There?" One of the doctors replied. "We left there a thousand years or so ago."

I contemplated the place that the scientists had bought me back from.

"Can I stay here?" I pleaded. I suppose this was a plea for my life.

"No. There is no room."

A haze appeared in my head.

Nothing.

"Can you hear me?"

"Uh?"

"Can you hear me?"

"Yes," I replied. They had bought me back!

I looked around me and I recognised this as a different place. It was a hospital ward, more obviously this time.

"Good." Said the doctor. " Can you hear me Mr. Richardson?

You've been in a coma for three months. You are really lucky. Your heart stopped beating for a while. It is a miracle you survived. I suppose you can't believe any of this eh Mr. Richardson?"

"Just tell me my name again"

"Signal"

Of course the conspiracy theorists had been correct all along.

Deliberately mislaid Government papers revealed the whole story. To many it didn't come as a surprise. The signals had been received for some fifteen years before the public got to hear anything about them. The scientists had to be sure they were genuine, had to crack the code and had to be certain of the "security" issues before the general public were informed.

Amazingly, with no attempt to cover up or deny the whole affair a press conference was quickly organised in front of packed bewildered journalists. The US president proudly announced to a shocked world that NASA scientists had been in receipt of coherent communications from another intelligent civilisation for quite some time. However, the public's excitement was soon dampened when government scientists announced that the signals were originating from a location some 20 light years from our own. This meant that, remarkably, the replies that had been sent would take at least 20 years to reach them.

Initially the signals were in the form of a speculative repeated radio pulse sent out comprising a simple number system. Later these were followed by a type of alphabet and then, formed from these systems, increasingly detailed information about a civilisation not unlike our own. The years taken to detect and unlock the code later frustrated Earth scientists as wasted time during which our replies could have been on their way. Many people felt that if only the government had funded this project properly, we would have saved five years at least. The broadcasts contained more information with each one that was decoded and began to include information about the current events of the alien civilisation. It was clear that the civilisation had so far discovered no other intelligent life.

The decision was made to reply to the alien broadcasts in a similar manner. Fortunately it did not take Earth scientists too long to pinpoint the origin of the signals.

They were disappointed when they realised the length of time it would take for their replies to reach their correspondents, so decided to include twice as much information in our replies.

The alien communications became more informative and detailed. Fascinated Earth scientists began to learn a lot about their new friends. It would still be quite a number of years until the aliens realised that they were not just broadcasting speculatively without response.

Their broadcasts were quite clear in the fact that the aliens had been making these broadcasts for many years in every direction and they were nearing conclusion in their theory that they were the only fishes in the sea.

If only they knew we were here, we were listening and we were replying.

After basic information about their biology, their environment, their history and culture, the broadcasts contained more specific details of their society.

The "news" broadcasts went on for years. They continued to tell of continued political unrest on their planet and preparations for an impending war. A highly advanced society such as theirs claimed to be capable of some pretty advanced weapons. By advanced they meant "powerful".

Their final broadcast solemnly declared in their language, that they were "now only a short time from imminent mutually assured destruction". This broke the hearts of Earth's scientists, and unanimously governments decided not to release that particular information to the general public although leaks were inevitable one day.

Sadly, our new friends were still one year away from receiving our first broadcast.

"Swansong"

"I need to speak to Darren urgently about these test results."

"I'm afraid he's gone missing Dr Taylor. He went out last night and has not come home. We are all rather worried." Replied Darren's mother.

Darren was over France by then on a budget plane ticket. He had his MP3 player on, was immersed in the new "Swansong" track and couldn't care less to say the least. He'd had enough.

"To Hell with it." Darren thought. "I've felt so rough for so long recently, I'm off to the sun before the summer is out."

So he'd packed his case, got his passport and without a word to anyone who loved him, headed to the airport by taxi. People his age always travelled light. He had a history of being unpredictable and had no responsibilities. It was just like him.

However, recently his parents would not even have allowed him to go to the corner shop on his own, such was the apparent state of his health.

Darren had begun feeling unwell a year ago. Oh yes, he knew something was wrong. He had lost weight, was in constant abdominal pain, was full of nausea and was incredibly tired all the time. Darren's previous riotous lifestyle did not help. His GP was reluctant to sympathise at first and was suspicious of "alternative" medications that may or may not have been taken by Darren. He had told the patient to stop drinking, to get more sleep and to take various painkillers and anti-depressants he prescribed. This advice proved all the more difficult to take for a twenty-four hour "work hard - play hard" party boy Darren. Exam stress was the doctor's temporary diagnosis while they were waiting for the results of yet another set of blood tests. As an attempt to make Darren regain his appetite, body weight and energy levels, his GP had prescribed a hefty cocktail of steroids, painkillers and antidepressants. Darren was simultaneously taking all these drugs and in rather large amounts. His pain did feel better, he had more energy, and to other people at least, he certainly looked a "lot more like it". So he tried to not worry about it so much.

"I really don't have the time to waste with all this." Thought the teenager as he walked out of the chemist the previous week.

His heart warmed as he squinted at the blinding glow of the sun above the cotton wool clouds. He would soon be approaching Ibiza. Summer was nearly over in the UK. He resolved to move to Spain permanently after university.

Darren was on the way to surprise some university mates who had managed to find a holiday job in the resort. That was exactly where Darren intended to have been all summer.

He checked into his hastily arranged budget hotel room then set about ringing around to try to locate the guys from university. By then, it was early evening but even the buildings and floors were reassuringly warm to the touch. "Excellent." Thought Darren as he removed his unnecessary United Kingdom garments of socks and jacket. The music was beginning to get louder in the bars beneath the hotel. He threw his case onto the small bed but had no intention of getting into it until sunrise the next day. The smell of pavement fish barbecues and Spanish lager wafted upward with the traffic fumes from the noisy road below. It was good to have fresh air. Oh, how those brought back memories.

Soon, due to the flight, he felt a bit rough again so he took a few more painkillers and tried to put it all to the back of his mind.

"This is more like it." Thought Darren as he treated himself to his first can of ice cool lager later that Friday night. It never tasted like that back home, especially on an empty stomach.

Socks removed and his single clean shirt on, Darren hit the town. Eventually, he managed to make contact with his barely-sober mates and arranged to call into the pub where they were working via a badly driven taxi.

To be honest he was only "Friends of friends" with these guys. He didn't care. They looked like they were enjoying themselves and gave him a loud and warm welcome. This was just what he wanted. To hell with everything.

Darren was soon introduced to some further friends of theirs and after a few lagers in the pub they ended up in a nightclub. The music was quite good that night. "Swansong" was played late into the night. Darren felt particularly hot. After a few icy Alco-pops and vodka shots, he was dancing away into his own world as the rest of the night blurred into a dream. As Darren felt the weight of all the troubles in his mind gently lifted he decided that this was exactly where he wanted to be.

He was being kissed. Who was that going to be? He couldn't remember. Somehow already knowing he was on the beach, he gradually woke to squint into the blur of the face of whoever was kissing him. He squirmed.

"Sod off..."

It was a little dog. Darren was on the beach and he was having his face licked by a dog. A little dog? It was not the wake-up call he had intended in the night before. He felt quite good considering the previous night and was not as hung-over as he usually got. It must have been the sea air.

The dog was a scruffy little puppy. He was rather emaciated and ribs protruded sharply. His eyes were disproportionately large and clear. The pup did not appear to be in a good way but he wagged his tail eagerly at Darren as he tilted his head from side to side. Darren softened a little.

"Go on. Get off..." Darren tried to shoo him away but he sat looking into Darren's eyes.

"Listen, I've got to head back to the hotel and get some kip before tonight." He told the mongrel.

He lay back. Everything felt pleasant at that moment. The warm wind was a fresh massage of silky air while the lapping of the sea on the rocks seemed to beat in a similar rhythm to his favourite song. Already, Darren turned his thoughts towards the night ahead. He would phone his parents to let them know he was all right.

The pup sat on his legs. Darren uncharacteristically felt sorry for him. He had never felt sorry for anything or anyone in life except for himself. He thought that the dog *did* look very hungry.

"OK. I'll find some breakfast for both of us then. Come on..."

Noticing the animal's difficulty walking steadily, Darren found himself carrying his new friend and found his way back to the hotel. Knowing full well that the hotel owner would in no way let a dog into the place, he wrapped the animal in a beach towel and smuggled him through reception without a problem. Fortunately no one was around.

The dog was not moving much and this concerned Darren more. He thought about calling a vet. The cost of a vet would be extortionate there and the last of Darren's student budget would be needed for kebabs and beer for the rest of the week.

Obviously starved and weak, Darren knew that stuffing the dog full of meat would do more harm than good. He began by giving him a little mineral water and then encouraged him to lap milk from his hand.

"Milk? I've never bought milk in my life. What's going on?"

The dog lay flat, panting and exhausted but soon found some relief in the shade on the tiles by Darren's open balcony window. Darren went out to buy something to make beef tea for the dog. Where had he heard about that? "Beef tea? How on earth…?"

When Darren got back with the supplies, he was concerned that the dog had made a turn for the worse. His eyelids and gums looked very pale and his short breaths moved rapidly. The dog also was too warm for his liking. Darren decided that he would have to stay around to nurse the little guy. In the morning he hoped the dog would be recovered so he could get rid of him and get on with the holiday. Darren, himself was feeling fine.

Rather than regretting missing the night out, he felt better knowing that Saturday evening he could keep an eye on the dog to who he felt a responsibility. He even found himself yelling at the crowd of revellers in the room below to keep the noise down so the patient could sleep.

"Keep the noise down? What's going on?" Thought Daniel. "People are usually shouting that at me."

In the morning, Darren found that his little roommate had somehow managed to crawl onto the bed in the night. This was a good sign.

Awake early, the pair of them sat on the balcony. The colours of the sunrise were matched by colour coming back into the skin of the tiny mongrel, who was no longer running a temperature.

Darren thought about the experience for the first time in his life and he couldn't remember the last time he had seen the sun rise to mark the actual *beginning* of a day after he had slept. Usually it was only ever seen as he staggered home from a very late night at a club.

By lunchtime, the pup felt like having a tug at Darren's shorts. By the evening, Darren was turning up his CD player to disguise the yelps of the pup, as he made busy with one of Darren's trainers. "You don't care about designer labels, do you little guy? Good for you!"

He took him for a walk that night or rather he carried him most of the way. He saw some guys from the club on Friday night. "Coming out later?" They asked

"Well, I'm looking after a mate. I had better have an early night" Replied Darren, motioning to the wriggling bundle in his shirt.

The revellers admired the pup, as did other people that night. He had made an improvised lead out of a trouser belt and some string and led him around the resort.

By next morning the young dog was regaining his strength and was walking quite freely. Darren got hold of a little chicken for them both but encouraged the dog to rest between his feeds.

Darren found that he was never short of company with this new companion. Groups of girls, in particular, freely approached the odd couple. Things didn't normally happen this way round for Darren.

He did visit the nightclub briefly again but drank only mineral water and left very early so as to check on the welfare of the new friend.

Rather than spend the daylight hours of the next ten days recovering from excesses as was usual, Darren spent time exploring the outdoors of the resort, taking simple pleasure in exploring and finding more about the actual history of the area. Before then he didn't learn anything except for the names of the best clubs. He spent a lot of time chatting to all manner of people who had stopped to admire his four-legged companion. By the end of the first week new friendships were being made, exams and health problems were forgotten about and the pair had become inseparable.

Darren and his dog were invited to play volleyball on the beach at the weekend. That was great fun. It had been a long time since he did any sport and it didn't tire him out.

Later, the two companions both fell asleep on the beach after a late sunset barbeque.

It had taken three days for the authorities to trace Darren's mother. She was called to Ibiza to identify a body found on a beach. He had apparently died of natural causes shortly after leaving a nightclub the previous Friday night, just hours after arriving on the island. A policewoman assured the distraught parents that Darren's face had seemed peaceful on the empty stretch of beach.

Later that day, Darren's parents visited the area where the body was found.

The beach had been closed to the public temporarily. Police tape cordoned off the area. The sole other inhabitant of the entire beach was a tiny stray puppy who watched with interest as he wobbled around.

"Progress"

Three steps. OK. Door closed. A waft of warm hotel air with a different scent and everything is behind me. Treading on the thin hotel carpet I glide along surprisingly efficiently down the twelfth floor corridor. A lift has its doors open in front of me at the end. I step inside alone, press the button for the ground floor and wait for the doors to close. Tick one, tick two, there we go. The elevator springs into silent motion as I fasten up my tie and straighten my jacket. I just know that my necktie will be out of line and my jacket lop-sided. I don't look into the reflective class on the walls. I don't like mirrors. When I see mirrors I see imperfections in myself and that causes extra work. I look up at the ceiling instead. One second, two seconds, three. Fifteen in all and the lift is already at the bottom. Maybe I did not think I would get this far. I wonder why not. As the door opens to reveal the busy lobby, people are getting on with their business. I don't want to hang around. A cab will be the quickest way home but I don't want to stand around, don't have a lot of cash and I don't feel like a conversation today. I walk straight outside into the warm evening air. Each step is progress. Each progressive step feels like it is moving my day forward to get another job ticked off. I step over the legs of a beggar, around a sandwich board man and across the park. I don't feel good about the park. It is too open. Twenty more steps I need. It turns out to be thirty- two in all. I had been counting my steps for so many years that I thought I was an accurate dab hand at getting my estimates spot on. Why was I so wide of the mark today? It was a different day than usual. I don't like "different". I like things to follow routine. I was a little flustered today. Wind passes my ears. That indicated motion and progress. That's good. I like to get things done. I see the entrance to the subway. Down I go onto the first step. That is progress and I move to the other world beneath the streets. It is a better world with neatly regimented floor and wall tiles and countable steps. The subway staircase is crowded. Good. I fold my coat sleeve over the handrail. I can never touch them. How many people have touched them today? I have been down this one a few times before. There are 73 steps to the bottom of this one with two more to follow just around the corner. I remembered this one. I don't like those new escalator things. I didn't feel like I am making progress down them and it was impossible to count exactly many steps there are on something that just would not stop moving. I knew it was a loop and I could work out the length but you see, I had to see all of the distinct pieces to convince myself completely that I can actually *count* them. I have to count them exactly and only then can I move on.

Otherwise there could always be just one or two out-of-site that would need counting. No, give me stairs any time. They are solid and easy. I can count them and then move on to get on with my day.

I look up at the clock on the station platform. Seven fourteen. Station clocks are fine with me because someone else has set them. I never wear a watch any more these days. I am never fully convinced that they are keeping the exact time. I spent so much time trying to synchronise my watches with all the other clocks and watches around that even my therapist finally gave up hope and told me to get rid of the "damned thing" and to never wear another. He was right. My turning up in his waiting room earlier and earlier each week prompted his decision. I don't like being late but being early is good so long as I am usefully using the time. Being late for appointments must be terrible a terrible thing to do and must make the offenders feel really guilty. It would be over two and a quarter minutes until 7:20 PM. I don't like waiting for trains. Some things I don't mind waiting for. I don't like people waiting for me, though.

I look up at the clock. It has a second hand to keep my concentration. I'm glad it wasn't one of those clean sweeping analogue ones. I don't want to think. I keep looking at the clock. I wonder who actually sets them. People begin to stand around me, all waiting for the same train. I don't mind being around people so long as they are in order. Those laces on that guy's shoes really need to be done up. I consider getting on another carriage than this guy with the laces; otherwise I'll spend the entire journey thinking about his shoes. Other than that I would be counting and double- counting the stops. Then I would be calculating the remaining journey time and double checking it against visible station clocks that I could see through the dirty train windows. Did no one ever clean those? Was it nobody's job? Could people go home from work and sleep at night knowing that those windows had not been cleaned? I remembered one night I got out of bed at 3 AM to wash my bike, after being unable to sleep. I began to think of my list of jobs at home for the weekend. My list was very full.

Three steps. Inside. A warm air waft while the doors close.

I end up sitting in my usual subway train seat position opposite one guy with his shirt collar curling unevenly up at the back. That would bug me now. Before therapy, I used to get into all sorts of trouble reacting to untidy problems with other people's clothes. You know the sort of thing. One shirt sleeve rolled up, one down, trousers curled up at the bottom, a single open button on a shirt or blouse. Dreadful. I can't live with it. Now you see why I don't like mirrors. I was told to convince myself that if I could not actually see the problem then the problem was not actually there and was not worth worrying about in the first place. In an attempt to rid me of this particular "condition", my therapist and my hypno-therapist at one point almost convinced me that the moon is not actually there when no one looks at it.

This OCD was a big problem for me. Would I ever be free of these obsessive-compulsive problems?

How long had I been doing this? How many millions of numbers had I counted? That wasn't an exaggerated figure pulled out of the air. I was quite accurate with my estimates, as you know. Just how many millions of numbers? I avoided seriously asking myself that very rhetorical question in case I decided to begin work to come up with an exact figure.

I often think back to the days before this all began and the toll it had taken upon my life. Why couldn't I have been obsessed with golf, sports cars, women or something altogether healthier? You see, I admit that I have a problem but can't seem to do anything about it, no matter what I try. In therapy, I had regressed through and through my earliest memories to find the trigger, the single origins of incidents that caused me to live the whole of my life in this unproductive wasted way.

Sixteen stops, eight and a half minutes journey time left and I finish counting momentarily while the train is delayed. Things are back in routine. Things are as they always are. I stare frustrated at that guy's still-upturned collar and the filthy train windows. I shuffle my tie and look at reflections in my shoe leather as I adjust my feet to make them exactly level. One thought breaks through the numbers, bothering me even more than the disarray and incompletion that I see around me.

I had decided to do something about my problems after all these years. Something that could give me an escape from this imprisonment and something more of a life without numbers. Was I expecting an instant cure? On my way home today, I realise that I am actually still counting after I had eliminated the root cause of the problem and was progressing into my new life. I didn't feel any better. I was still counting. The train starts moving again and I look at the nearest station clock. I begin to become annoyed at the abacus toy on the front of a child's pushchair. The counters need all to be pushed to the left. Not just some of them. I try not to look at it.

The root cause of the problem lay neatly cold on a hotel room couch with their throat slit open.

"Acquired Taste"

We'd almost cracked it. I say "Almost". At that point we'd very nearly stamped out smoking once and for all. This wasn't just the result of the Government whacking up duty on tobacco again and again to simply price the things out of the market. That just succeeded in moving cigarettes over into the black market. At least within the legal market we could at least regulate the ingredients to some extent. In the black and grey markets where large quantities of contraband tobacco was bought and sold in pubs and car boot sales heaven only knew what some of those blends contained. There were already some 400 potentially harmful compounds in a cigarette without adding any more.

New anti-smoking laws did help and the number of legitimate smoking areas became very few and far between. Offenders stood out and were named and shamed. There were by then electronic cigarette detectors everywhere. Smokers would get caught out in the most remote of locations and became the subject of much ridicule. Many a true word was said in jest and it did literally mean that climbing a mountain or sailing to the centre of an ocean soon became the only options for those still with "the addiction". And then for legal reasons if there were any non-smokers around the mountaintop or boat then there would be a risk of litigation.

Health professionals including myself thought that teenage girls would be the hardest demographic group to crack. We had driven the propaganda message home with blitz of graphic gory attrition in schools about how much cosmetic damage cigarettes could actually do to their long-term appearance. All this was in addition to the simple injection made available freely that basically overrode the addictive effects of nicotine. Given alongside the usual inoculations, most parents were keen for their children to have this "immunisation".

Previously, people with "the addiction" were sitting ducks as a source for Governments' badly needed tax revenue. Secretly, Government ministers mumbled about their loss of tax income but they were persuaded that they would ultimately recoup some of this by savings on expensive long-term treatment of terminal smoking related diseases.

When the teenage girls were sorted, we were very nearly done. There was just the one single group that we couldn't get off the drug no matter how hard we tried. We looked forward to the day when we had essentially ended the "addiction" once and for all and the manufacturers would be completely out of any viable business.

The stubborn problem came predominantly from men around forty to forty-five years old. Initially, I thought that a peak of stress levels among working middle-age males was the reason behind this stubbornness, and I was part of a new Government-funded study group set up to investigate ways to remedy this particular problem. The strange thing was that this was a worldwide initiative and the UK was now the last country in Europe to have a significant smoking problem amongst any particular demographic. It seemed that this very sector just would not stop buying cigarettes for neither love nor money. Most of them smoked on average four packs a day and most of the cigarettes were a particular brand, made by a company called Rodeo who had been around for about fifty years. The men were still buying the things quite happily despite pressures from all directions. Admittedly, Rodeo complied with regulations for displaying the required warnings and they were still making a profit in their niche market. Their customers came from all walks of society and from all socio-economic groups.

For me, the strange thing was that they didn't show the usual nicotine withdrawal cravings. In fact, they didn't show the usual addictive traits of chain smokers at all. Bizarrely, some seemed to have merely stockpiled large quantities of un-smoked packets of the things. However, what they *did* seem to show was more of a purchasing addiction. They felt the need to *buy* pack after pack of the things day after day. I was convinced that the answer lay within the actual sales behaviour of Rodeo.

The company had always spent a great deal of time and effort on its commercials, albeit under increasingly restrictive Government guidelines. Their adverts were catchy, masculine and had a hardedge to their imagery and soundtrack. They were appreciated even by non-smokers for their artistic merit. But when other tobacco companies had flattered them by following a similar style of advertising they didn't reap anything like the same level of commercial success as Rodeo.

We spent a lot of time studying in-depth a couple of heavy smokers who were addicted to Rodeo cigarettes. They were keen to earn extra cash, no doubt to spend on their addiction. We needed to know exactly why this was still happening in this day and age. Why hadn't this group in particular become addicted to any other brand and why when we could medically remove the nicotine addiction from the equation did these guys just keep on buying pack after pack? These were otherwise rational and intelligent men.

I needed to know Rodeo's trick. So, I looked more deeply into the background history of the company rather than the customers'. I found all the usual stuff. I looked at their directors and senior staff. Most were the usual kind of people involved in that industry and the company was a family owned business that had been handed down for at least two generations.

Then the Internet came into itself.

I gained a tremendous lot of information quickly from the many social networking web sites. I just knew I would find a use for them one day. Gradually, I began to piece together a possible direction. It is amazing just what a trail of evidence can be left on the web for all to see if one takes the time to look for it. A few years ago Rodeo Tobacco had undergone the sector's drop in sales, in common with their whole industry. But then six months further on they began to buck the overall trend and make up ground. They began to arrogantly ride their unique wave of loyal sales in a way that had everyone baffled. I sifted through more and more information still from the company reports. I needed to discover if there were any significant changes to the company around the particular time that it began to turn things around.

I formed a chronology of company events and began to look back a year before that, looking particularly at the comings and goings of personnel.

One of the directors of the company had married for the second time. Again, from information freely available on social networking websites I was even able to obtain photos of that particular event. She had married a man known as D.D.Hampshire. A significant fact for me was that he had been quickly given a well-paid job on their sales team soon after the wedding. "Jobs for the boys" as they say and it had certainly done the company no harm. As I searched in detail through the backgrounds of each of the directors and the managers in turn, it was D.D.Hampshire's that was the most intriguing appointment of them all. His background seemed inappropriate. Hampshire was not from a commercial background. Instead, he had been involved in various artistic careers for most of his fairly innocuous working life. Studying drama and art at university, he had first found work in the seventies with a regional South-East TV company. One connection led to another and he got involved in children's television. During his time there he became closely involved in the production of one of those obscure mid-seventies children's television animations called

"Grippers". This was the sort of programme that kids enjoy immensely at the time, and then forget forever more until it crops up out-of-the-blue for a brief moment years later. It was to be D.D.Hampshire's one-and-only claim to fame. So, off at a tangent, I read further about this strange little series. It was an off-beat (and literally) hard-hitting boys' after-school series based on loud, violent Plasticene models which were just perfect for its target audience and their dads alike if they were home at that time. Running for just nine episodes, "Grippers" never made it to a second series probably due the changing social climate of the time. However, in its day, it became a short-lived cult playground favourite spawning a small army of devotees who could quote every line of dialogue verbatim and mimic the theme tune before repeatedly punching someone's shoulder. Nowadays, that particular TV show was long forgotten and there was very little trace of it left even on the deepest of Internet searches. Recipients' memories of the punches were not forgotten apparently, judging by some victims' accounts written on various other Internet support groups. Seemingly the original master tapes and scripts of the show had been long mislaid and that was all in the days long before home video recording. Unlike many other childhood favourites of the time, it had never been re-released in any form of media since then, so I never got to see any actual footage. The lines, characters and slogans of the show were to remain only a deeply buried memory within its one-time fans. My only recollection of that show was that I could remember its name cropping up in a difficult pub quiz a few years ago. Well before my time, this was a tenuous connection but I did wonder if our two sample smokers remembered it. They were indeed "Seventies boys". And they were seventies boys from a single television region of the UK. The show was never exported. Further research suggested there were unproved allegations that "Grippers" was bursting full of double entendres and subliminal imagery. Through the Internet, I soon got hold of a dusty home-recorded audiotape cassette of one episode. I played it in a friend's old car.

Bingo.

The squeaky voiced chain-smoking "Brown Gripper" character seemed to never remove the fag from his mouth even when continually slamming another character's head on a kitchen table....accompanied by music....accompanied by a simple melody........accompanied by the same melody used within the brief score played behind Rodeo's cigarette commercials. Then there were the words contained in the clever slogans from the cigarette posters. Re-arranged slightly and they were right out of "Brown Gripper's" best catch phrases.

Bingo. Got you.

Our two smokers remembered the series well "now that they came to think about it"

Now came the next task. I had to prove that Hampshire knew exactly what he was doing and to find out if had he broken any laws. A good lawyer could sort that out.

I phoned the lawyer.

He hadn't broken any laws in the Rodeo commercials but he would soon be in all sorts of serious retrospective legal trouble for the "influence of subliminal content on minors".

Biographical Notes

Steve is a peripatetic teacher of maths and science. He travels around his region teaching seriously ill children who can't get to school and values his job very highly.

Despite a background in mathematics and science, one major part of Steve's life is his love of quality English literature. He collects and owns many classic first editions.

He will be ever grateful to his parents who taught him to read fluently at the age of four.

Short story writing began in his school days where he enjoyed winning the literature prize.

With a head readily spawning original (and sometimes randomly bizarre) short stories, Steve's move out of the classroom has given him time to enjoyably type them up. Stories that had their origins in Steve's teenage years began to find their way into anthologies and magazines. A lifelong ambition for him has always been to author a book traditionally into print. He often dreamed of seeing a full paperback of his own work on a bookshop shelf.

Steve graduated in maths from Manchester Metropolitan University in 1993, after representing them in soccer for four years. He then taught in schools in Surrey, Staffordshire and Cheshire.

With no family and few relatives, Steve places great value on his close friendships.

He also enjoys contributing to magazine articles, horticulture, DIY, his little sports car, art, bookbinding and photography. He also confesses to following his free-falling league 2 soccer team.

He lives in a rural location in South Cheshire accompanied by a guardian of a dog.

Lightning Source UK Ltd.
Milton Keynes UK
04 June 2010

155072UK00002B/141/P